OCT 1 5 2005

MYSTERY / MCI

IRISH
GILT

IRISH
GILT

RALPH McINERNY

 St. Martin's Minotaur ≋ New York

www.minotaurbooks.com

Library of Congress Cataloging-in-Publication Data

McInerny, Ralph M.
    Irish gilt / Ralph McInerny.—1st U.S. ed.
      p. cm.
    ISBN-13: 978-0-312-33688-2
    ISBN-10: 0-312-33688-8
    1. Knight, Roger (Fictitious character)—Fiction. 2. Knight, Philip (Fictitious character)—Fiction. 3. Private investigators—Indiana—South Bend—Fiction. 4. Zahm, John Augustine, 1851–1921—Influence—Fiction. 5. University of Notre Dame—Fiction. 6. Gold mines and mining—Fiction. 7. South Bend (Ind.)—Fiction. 8. College teachers—Fiction. I. Title.

PS3563.A31166I644 2005
813'.54—dc22

                                   2005047015

First Edition: October 2005

10 9 8 7 6 5 4 3 2 1

For Chris and Jen Kaczor

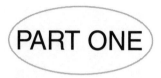

PART ONE

FOOL'S GOLD

1 APRIL WAS THE CRUELEST MONTH for Philip Knight. The basketball season was over, including the bookstore tournament; the hockey schedule was complete; baseball lay in the future, as did spring football practice. Bleak weeks without the diversion of Notre Dame sports confronted him.

"They might as well shut the place down, Roger."

"You could sit in on a few classes."

Philip gave him a cold eye. "Yours?"

"No, no, I didn't mean mine."

"What's this?" Phil asked, picking up a sheaf of stapled pages.

"My syllabus."

Phil waited.

"An outline of the course."

"So students know where you're going?"

"Not just the students."

Roger was giving a course on the life and writings of the once famous Father John Zahm, now all but forgotten on the campus where he had been a massive presence in the late nineteenth and early twentieth centuries. Poor Phil had probably already heard enough about Zahm right here in their apartment.

"I could take a vacation, I suppose."

"Where would you go?"

For a moment there was a spark in Phil's eye as possibilities occurred to him, but soon the spark went out. "I don't want to go on vacation."

"Of course not. Who would want to leave Notre Dame?"

Not Roger Knight, certainly. Since his appointment several years ago to the Huneker Chair in Catholic Studies, he felt that his life had become a vacation. He had a magnificent library at his disposal; he had the university archives in which to wallow; he offered courses in whatever struck his fancy and was blessed with bright and interested students. Nonetheless, he could sympathize with Phil. When they moved to Notre Dame, Phil had sharply reduced the workload of his already very selective private investigations agency, the better to devote himself to the athletic seasons of the university. Now April had come, though, and the immediate prospect was a period without sports.

"Golf?"

"It's too soon. This is northern Indiana, you know."

"If you had a client . . ."

Phil had always selected his cases carefully, but he had never before thought of them as going on vacation.

"Phil, you might write your memoirs."

Phil leapt to his feet. "I think I'll go work out."

Roger nodded, as if in approval. The fact was that he regarded exercise as frivolous, particularly in its current almost religious form. "The aim is now dubbed wellness. I suppose it's not the first time an adverb was transformed into a substantive." That was the extent of his musings on the matter.

Phil fled, but not to exercise. Under the outgoing president, Monk Malloy, a dozen buildings had gone up that might have served as the priest's monument, but perhaps he thought the massive exercise center was his real claim to a permanent place in the institutional memory. There, at any hour of the day and well into the night, students and faculty and alumni huffed and puffed as they pointlessly trod treadmills with earphones clamped to their heads, going nowhere with a teleological grimace on their sweating faces. Glazed eyes peered into a future where a trim and agile self awaited. Such strenuous activity, unrelated to any athletic contest, struck even Phil as manic. He did look in, but only for a minute or two. Then he went on to the Loftus Center and Lefty Smith, the former hockey coach whose twilight years were devoted to managing the lesser exercise center that catered to the elderly and townspeople. Bald, balloonlike, and gentle as only one who had played a vicious sport could be, Lefty seemed the Before in an advertisement for getting in shape.

"Here he is!" Lefty cried when Phil looked into the office, which was filled with trophies and photos and other memorabilia. "This is Phil Knight."

A man who had occupied a chair across from Lefty's desk rose. His body had the deferential bent of a very tall man. "Boris Henry." He put out his hand, and Phil took it. A former hockey player?

Henry laughed when Phil put this thought into words. "Student manager. I tried out as a walk-on."

"Skate-on," Lefty corrected. Confidingly to Phil, he added, "Weak ankles."

Phil took a chair and listened to a recital of the seasons during which Henry had been student manager of the hockey team. He and Lefty seemed determined to top one another's memories. How could accounts of his old cases compete with stories like these? It was nearing noon, and Lefty suggested that they adjourn to the University Club for lunch.

At the club, they descended into the dining room and followed the rhythmic passage of Debbie, the hostess, among the tables, under the arched ceiling, to a table near the bar where aging jocks and athletic enthusiasts congregated daily. Ray Brach and Roland Kelly were already in place at the round table, which had been dubbed, ironically, the Algonquin Table by the late Jim Carberry. Phil sat down next to Henry and asked him what brought him back to campus.

"Nostalgia."

Phil nodded. The loyalty of Notre Dame alumni was legendary and increased exponentially with former athletes.

"What do you know of Father Zahm?" Henry asked, ignoring the wider conversation.

"Zahm?" Phil looked warily at Henry. Had he been put up to this line of talk? But how could Lefty know what Roger was currently teaching? Al Syewczyk had arrived, and no one else seemed to have heard Henry over the increasing banter.

"I've heard of him."

Henry launched into an impassioned paean of praise for John Zahm, CSC, a giant of a priest a century ago. Zahm had lost a legendary quarrel about the direction of the university and had receded into writing and adventure. "He and Teddy Roosevelt were like that," Henry said, bringing two fingers together.

Phil was wary. He had not escaped the apartment in the expectation of running into a Zahm enthusiast. It was Henry's conviction that Notre Dame had not done enough to honor the priest.

"Isn't there a hall named after him?"

Henry made a face. "A residence hall! How can that possibly be sufficient honor for such a renaissance man? There should be a Zahm Institute, a collection of all his books and papers, a special library, fellowships . . ."

"You should talk to my brother."

A look of puzzlement formed on Henry's face and then faded. "Knight!" he said. "Are you related to Roger Knight?" If Henry had been intense before learning that Phil and Roger were brothers, he now became truly excited. "I have to meet him."

Phil caught Lefty's eye, but the coach's expression told him nothing. Had this been arranged? Throughout the lunch, Henry babbled in Phil's ear, excluding him from the more interesting talk of the others. The only escape lay in promising to introduce Boris Henry to Roger.

2 LINES OF STUDENTS CAME AND went to classes in DeBartolo throughout the day, ants picking up and carrying away such crumbs of learning as were dispensed there. As he approached the classroom building, Josh Daley's step quickened at the sight of a swishing ponytail on the crowded walk before him. It was attached to the beautifully molded head of Rebecca de Vega Nobile, Beatrice to his aching heart, Laura to his sad, unsent efforts to convey to her in poetry his exalted feelings. Before he could reach her, several young men vied for the privilege of holding the door open for her. She swept regally in, blessing the victor with a smile, and then was gone.

Inside the building himself, Josh took the stairs to the second floor and shouldered his way through student traffic to the room where the class in Continental epistemology met. Continental epistemology! Josh found the course baffling. He had signed up for it when he overheard Rebecca announcing that she was enrolling in the course. Josh's major was history. Abstractions sailed over his head; he wanted anecdotes and events, the reassuring facts of actions and great deeds. Only infatuation could explain his suffering through lectures on the continuing influence of the Cartesian cogito on European thought. The class was taught by a mumbling bearded philosopher named Tenet, whose half-audible drone made Josh feel like an eavesdropper.

At the door of the classroom, he surveyed the rows of desks that descended toward the lectern where Tenet was shuffling papers, from time to time glancing at the clock that would digitally inform him to begin. Rebecca, as usual, was in the first row. She followed the lectures as if the course exceeded all her expectations. It was the rare meeting in which she did not raise a question that sent Tenet off on a tangent of irrelevancy. Josh pushed along the second row and sat behind her with an air of triumph. She did not know he existed. She did not know that she was the reason for his taking this penitential course. Scenarios in which he would introduce himself provided material for saving daydreams during Tenet's drivel.

The clock clicked, and Tenet began the lecture with a question. "Who of you knows of the Treaty of Westphalia?"

Josh straightened in his seat. The Treaty of Westphalia! Without thinking, he raised his hand. Tenet seemed startled, as if his question had been meant to be rhetorical. He consulted the mug shots on the lectern. "Daley?"

"Yes, sir."

"And what was the Treaty of Westphalia?"

Among other things, it was the subject of Josh's senior thesis. He rattled off a brief account of the treaty that had ended the religious wars of Europe.

Something happened to Tenet's beard. He seemed to be smiling. "And who were the signatories?"

For ten minutes there was an exchange between the profes-

9

sor and this knowledgeable student. Josh was wholly at ease because he was scarcely conscious that it was he who was holding forth in this course on Continental epistemology. In the row ahead of him, Rebecca turned, and her great green eyes looked at him with curiosity and admiration. Suddenly, Josh was brought back to himself and to the preposterous fact that he was speaking up in a philosophy course. It was history that was the issue, though, and history was his bailiwick.

The exchange ended with Tenet thanking Josh and then beginning to lecture on the significance for modern philosophy of the treaty. Rebecca now gave her rapt attention to the professor. Josh sat back and let the unintelligible mumble flow over him. He could scarcely believe what he had done. Most incredible of all had been the admiring glance of Rebecca.

Tenet ended his lecture when the digital clock on the wall told him that he had done his duty by this class. To teach undergraduates pained him. He needed the sophisticated response of graduate students, apprentice philosophers themselves, would-be peers. Undergraduate courses attracted the most curious mix of students, their choice more often than not dictated by the hour at which a class was taught. If he could have roused himself for the task, Tenet would have offered undergraduate classes in the first morning period, avoided by most students. Colleagues who did this told alluring stories of having only a handful of students, all of them philosophy majors. But Tenet read late into the night and was as much a stranger to morning as most students.

"Daley," he called, as the class was dispersing.

"Sir?"

"What is your major?"

"History."

"Ah." Tenet gathered his papers and shuffled away.

Rebecca stood and turned to Josh. She thrust out her hand. "Rebecca."

"Josh."

"Daley?"

"Yes."

They left together, but it was only when they were outside the building that they could talk.

"I love that class," she said.

"I've never had anything like it."

"I know."

"You're a philosophy major?"

"Of course."

"What hall are you in?" As if he didn't know. He wandered around Walsh so much he might have been arrested for stalking.

"Walsh. What's yours?"

"St. Ed's."

Her green eyes filled with approval. She hated the new halls. The fact that they both lived in historic residences seemed a link between them. They went on to Recker's for coffee, where she said, "If you like Tenet, you would love Roger Knight."

His major should have prepared him for the way in which the expected is overwhelmed by the actual outcome. None of the imaginary scenarios in which he had made himself known to Rebecca had been like this. She actually seemed to think he had a mind. He asked who Roger Knight was.

"The best thing since Joe Evans."

"Joe Evans?"

"Ask your father. He was a Domer, wasn't he?"

"Oh, yes."

The important thing was to say as little as possible, lest she discover how untypical his exchange with Tenet was. Or to divert the conversation.

"Why de Vega?"

She sat back, looking at him with a little smile. "How did you know?"

He shrugged. "I always check out who's in a class with me."

She accepted that. "Lope de Vega," she said.

"Ah."

"The Spanish poet. My father's nuts about him. He has everything he ever wrote."

"In Spanish?"

"Castilian."

"What's he like?"

"My father?" She looked away. Josh had meant Lope de Vega, whoever he was. She brightened. "But who am I to complain? It was my middle name that caught Roger Knight's attention. Of course, he knew all about Lope de Vega." It wasn't a criticism.

He walked her to Walsh, suddenly almost at ease. "Are you taking a course from Knight?"

She looked at him. "If you want to sit in, he wouldn't mind."

"When is it?" She told him. Well, he could skip his theology class. "Where is it?"

"Why don't you meet me here?"

"Good idea."

She nodded and smiled. "I hope so."

3 ⤑ ROGER KNIGHT SAT ON THE PATIO
of Holy Cross House with Father Car-
mody, his golf cart in the parking lot on the opposite side of
the building, enjoying the thin April sunlight with the old
priest. It was thanks to Father Carmody that Roger was at
Notre Dame, but it was more than gratitude that brought him
on his regular visits. Their conversations were a species of
oral history. By means of them, Roger had acquired a deeper
feeling for the past of the university, since Carmody had
been a man behind the scenes for most of his active career at
Notre Dame, an éminence grise even before his red hair had
turned white. Across the lake, the dome on the Main Building sparkled in the sunlight. Carmody was saying that the
statue of Our Lady on top of the dome was modeled after the
one Pope Pius IX had erected in the Piazza di Spagna in
Rome.

"Of course, it's larger." He meant Notre Dame's.

"How tall?"

"Sixteen feet."

The statue, like the dome, was golden. Father Carmody told
the story. After the fire of 1879, the Main Building had been
rebuilt, and in 1886 the first gilding took place. It was re-

newed periodically, at irregular intervals. The last time had been 1988.

"Real gold?"

"Oh, yes. Twenty-three-and-three-quarter-karat Lefranc Italian gold leaf."

"How do you remember such things?"

"I oversaw the process in 1988. It was done by the Conrad Schmitt Studios from New Berlin, Wisconsin."

"Expensive?"

Father Carmody opened his hands. "Father Sorin never spared expense to honor Our Lady, nor should we."

The bird feeder at the edge of the patio was alive with birds. A cardinal swooped in and scattered the others.

"They must be mere bishops," the old priest murmured.

"Of course, you didn't know Father Zahm."

"Just his brother Albert. He spent his last years here." The old priest wrinkled his nose. "Unlike Father Zahm."

"He was a brilliant man."

"We have never had his like again. But he wasn't a team player. Unless he was captain. He left when he wasn't reelected provincial and settled at our college in Washington, D.C."

"Settled?"

Father Carmody smiled. "Oh, he was already quite a traveler while he was here. How is your class going?"

"Wonderfully. How could the kids not be interested? I am emphasizing the range of his interests—science, of course, but seemingly everything else. Dante, the conquistadores, the Southwest. The reading list of one hundred great books he drew up for students is remarkable."

"I didn't know about that."

"You can find it in Weber's biography."

"I've always meant to read that."

"He acknowledges your help."

"Does he?"

"What was his brother Albert like?"

"He became quite distinguished. Most of his career was spent elsewhere, but, as I said, he came back here during his last years. He is one of the few laymen to be buried in the community cemetery."

"I am going to stop there on the way home."

Father Carmody stirred. "I'd like to come with you."

So it was that, in Roger's golf cart, they bumped across the lawn to Moreau Seminary and continued on to the community cemetery. Roger parked his cart on a pathway, and they got out. For the next hour, they wandered among the identical crosses marking the graves of the departed members of the Congregation of Holy Cross. At the southern end, in the shadow of a crucifix, lay Father Edward Sorin, and nearby was the grave of John Augustine Zahm.

"He was a great favorite of Sorin's," the old priest said.

"They visited the Holy Land together. Of course, Zahm wrote a book about it."

"Of course. Was that under one of his pseudonyms?"

"No." Zahm had published some books under an anagram of his name, H. J. Mozans, as well as under the names A. H. Johns and A. H. Solis. "Why did he use pseudonyms?"

"Modesty?"

Albert Zahm's grave was at the north end of the cemetery.

16

Father Carmody, as he had at every grave at which they stopped, traced the sign of the cross over himself and stood for a moment in silence. When he turned to look back the way they had come, he said, "I will be buried among youngsters."

"This place always reminds me of Arlington Cemetery." Row after row of identical crosses moved away from the grave of the founder.

"It's older."

Roger smiled. It was a Notre Dame kind of remark.

He dropped Father Carmody at Holy Cross House and continued to his apartment, where he found Phil waiting for him.

"Roger, this is Boris Henry."

The visitor rose from his chair, unfolding his body as he did, but remaining stooped. "This is indeed a privilege." He thrust out his hand. "I understand we share an interest in Father John Zahm."

"Ah."

Phil had not risen from the beanbag chair that held rather than supported him. Getting out of it was a bit of a trick, a trick Phil now performed, rolling to one side, getting a palm on the floor, and then levering himself awkwardly to his feet. "I'll leave you two alone."

"Mr. Henry and I can talk in the study, Phil."

"Boris," Henry said.

"Boris."

Phil dropped back into the beanbag and reached for the remote. Roger led Boris Henry into his office, where the tall man stood and looked wonderingly around, at the walls of books, at the computer, at the special chair that accommodated Roger's bulk and enabled him to wheel rapidly from desk to bookshelves.

"Marvelous," Henry said, then took the chair Roger indicated. "Your brother tells me that you're giving a course on Zahm."

"That's right."

"Tell me about it."

Boris Henry nodded enthusiastically through Roger's abbreviated account of what he was doing in the class. Finally, he sat back.

"Now let me tell you what I would like the university to do." There were a number of recently established centers at Notre Dame—Henry was all for them—and, of course, among them was what he called the granddaddy of them all, the Maritain Center. "Jacques Maritain was a great man. It is only fitting that he should be commemorated in that way. But, Roger, he was never on the faculty here. He was a guest lecturer at most. John Zahm *was* Notre Dame. He *is* what this place should be. You can see where my thoughts are heading."

"Tell me."

"A John Zahm Center, of course! Think of the variety of things it could foster—the relation of religion and science, science and literature, the moral responsibilities of scientists. The role of the Southwest in the history of the Church in this country. And he was a pioneer in what is now called women's studies." Boris paused. "To say nothing of his interest in the conquistadores and El Dorado."

18

"I think it is a great idea."

"His books are out of print, Roger. Why not a collected edition?"

"Convincing me is easy, of course, but you must talk to someone in the administration."

"That is the purpose of my visit. I have an appointment with the provost tomorrow. May I mention your enthusiasm for the idea?"

"For what good it might do."

"Of course, it will cost money, but surely money is no problem for Notre Dame."

4   ➤ THE ARCHIVES OF THE UNIVERSITY
of Notre Dame are located on the sixth
floor of Hesburgh Library, a cornucopia of papers, memorabilia, and publications on which any history of the university or of any of its various personnel and aspects must be based. There, for some days, in a glassed-in workroom, sat Xavier Kittock, class of '74, poring over the contents of gray archival boxes. On the table was a laptop computer, carefully placed so that no one who entered the room could learn of the project that engaged him. Secrecy was essential. Like other scholars obsessed with an idea, Kittock was certain that hordes of rivals were gathering to rob him of his subject. Surely there were dozens of others to whom his great idea had occurred. It was a matter of anguish to Kittock that the minions of the archives must know what he was up to. It was to lessen the danger of discovery that he dealt only with one archivist, Greg Walsh, a shy man whose speech impediment suggested that he would be unable to communicate Kittock's secret.

It was a phone call from Clare in Kansas City that explained Kittock's haste and secrecy. "Boris has gone to Washington," she had told him when she called the previous day. "He plans to stop at Notre Dame on the way back."

No need for her to spell out what that meant. Had Boris returned to Washington in the manner of one who, having found a gold coin, returned to the spot in the hope of finding more? It was in Washington that he had bought at auction a lot that proved to contain a travel diary of John Zahm's.

"Do you think he intends to give it to Notre Dame?" Kittock asked her.

"I think he hopes to sell it to them."

"Of course." Some time ago, Clare had given him the surprising news of Boris's personal financial embarrassment. Thanks to Clare, the rare book business, sequestered from Boris's own finances, flourished, but it was not money tree enough to support Boris's gambling.

"Have you found anything?" Clare asked.

"Not really."

His wild hope had been that the information that was surely contained in the diary Zahm had kept during the travels on which his two volumes on the conquistadores and his later one on El Dorado had been based would be found among the Zahm papers. The only hope now seemed to be the diary Boris had come into possession of, and all the ass could think of was some immediate profit from it. For Kittock it represented far more.

The adventurers of an earlier time had spawned a new kind of adventurer. Tales of sunken Spanish galleons full of gold had inspired expeditions to find and raise that long-lost treasure, and some had succeeded. Kittock had invested in one such expedition and spent some months with the visionary and his crew off the coast of South America. The expedition had not been a success, but others had been. How much treasure had been spent in the quest for such treasure? It was the source of the gold that had come to interest Kittock, especially the legend of El Dorado. At least two places had been thought to mark the site of that city of gold. Zahm had been to both, and it was Kittock's conviction that the priest had learned that the object of the quest of so many did exist.

Clare was unconvinced. "However much he admired those who sought it, he laments their greed."

Kittock nodded. "Cupidity was his favorite word. The later popular account is even more moralizing. That was a screen."

"I think the gold bug has bit you."

But it was Cupid rather than cupidity that had come to his aid with Clare. The first time he tugged her to him, she had come easily into his arms.

"I can't believe you never married," he said.

"Neither did you."

"The navy kept me busy, and a war or two."

"Maybe I've been waiting."

If she had been, it must have been for Boris. Her boss was a widower, and she was his good right arm; she was a very attractive woman, and Boris, after all, was a man. But apparently nothing had happened. Was there an undercurrent of resentment in Clare because of that? As their friendship deepened, it became clear to Kittock that her loyalty to Boris Henry did in fact have bounds. Perhaps Kittock would marry Clare. For the moment, he seemed to be using her. Their alliance was sealed when she called to tell him about Boris's great find in Washington, the South American travel diary of John Zahm.

Kittock had flown from his home in Florida to Kansas City and exulted with his old roommate in his find. "Let me see it."

"Maybe later."

Later never came, and this had fueled Kittock's hunch. Perhaps the two of them, he and Clare, could become partners in the venture.

"He hasn't a cent to invest," Clare said.

"He has the diary."

"Yes."

"Have you looked at it?"

She dipped her chin. "No."

"Don't you have access to the rare book vault at the store?"

"It isn't there. It's in a safe-deposit box at his bank."

Kittock knew a moment of panic. Had Boris been struck by the same epiphany he had? Kittock had on previous visits mentioned the expedition he had gone on.

"Sunken gold?" Boris had been skeptical.

"Some has been found."

"Treasure Island," Boris said dismissively. At the time he seemed to find the whole idea fantastic, but he could have had second thoughts. Now, his intention to visit Notre Dame on his return from Washington suggested that Boris had in mind a more immediate return on his investment. Investment! He had bought the box containing the diary for fifty dollars.

How had such a precious item ended up in such a box? Well, first, it hadn't been recognized as precious. As far as

Kittock could guess, getting rid of the box along with many other things had been a result of the madness that had seized many religious houses after the Council. From Clare he had learned that many seminary libraries had ended up in bookstores all across the country, books gotten rid of with abandon on the assumption that nothing they contained was relevant anymore. Now, of course, there was a brisk trade in such items. Holy Cross College in Washington, where Zahm had lived after leaving Notre Dame in 1906 after his stormy term as provincial, was not exempt from this madness. After his death, many of Zahm's books would have ended up in the library there or in boxes consigned to the attic. Had anyone even opened the box before the auction? Actually, it had been called a garage sale.

After two days in the archives, it had been impossible to avoid the curiosity of Greg Walsh.

"If I knew what you were after, I could be of more help." The archivist managed to stammer this out.

So Kittock told him a story. Walsh would know of Weber's life of Zahm. "It was originally his doctoral dissertation," Kittock reminded him.

Walsh nodded. "It is a marvelous book."

"I am thinking of a life of Zahm for kids," Kittock told him.

The idea was prompted by an experience Kittock had had in the campus bookstore on a visit last fall. On game days, anything not nailed down could be sold to the visiting fans. At a table in the hallway, a woman author was signing copies of her book. Kittock drew near. He looked over the shoulder of a lady who had just purchased the book. Book! The pages were of thick cardboard, perhaps a dozen in all. There was a Notre Dame slogan on each illustrated page. It might have been the product of a few days' work, and here it was, selling like popcorn. Kittock wandered away, brooding.

Walsh seemed to find the idea of a life of Zahm for young adults plausible. "Good luck with it."

"Kids would be particularly fascinated by his accounts of El Dorado."

Walsh couldn't agree more. "There are letters, too, you know."

Kittock wished he had thought of the excuse of a book earlier. Walsh proved very helpful now that he knew what sort of thing Kittock was after. Letters written from South America to Zahm's brother Albert seemed to contain hints of what Kittock was sure would be found in the diary.

He went to Grace Hall for lunch and was seated at an outdoor table pretending that spring had come when Greg Walsh joined him.

"Okay?"

"Sure. Of course." Kittock was not pleased. He ate lunch here most days and had come to believe that his interest in one of the waitresses was returned.

Walsh seemed to speak more easily if he did so while chewing. It was the first thing approaching a conversation Kittock had ever had with the archivist. He was telling Kittock that Roger Knight was giving a course on Zahm.

"Really?"

"A crowded field. Do you know a man named Boris Henry?"

Kittock looked warily at the masticating archivist. "Why do you ask?"

"Another Zahm enthusiast."

"Why do you say that?"

Because Boris Henry had called the archives, asking after the Zahm holdings. "He's coming this afternoon. You can meet him."

"We were roommates."

Thank God for the warning. Back at the archives, Kittock gathered his materials and took the stairway to the main floor, not wanting to risk running into Henry in the elevator. Outside, he took a circuitous route to his car. He thought of going to the Grotto and lighting another candle. To fend off evil.

5   ➤   BORIS HENRY HAD MARRIED WELL, the daughter of a senior partner—an equivocal blessing, since this seemed to lock him forever into the dull work of the law.

Max Munson had looked over his prospective son-in-law with controlled enthusiasm. "School?"

"Notre Dame."

The frown disappeared and Munson beamed. That had been the open sesame. Dorothy, too, had gone to school in South Bend, but she and Boris had not known one another as students. They had met at a tennis club in Kansas City. The Munsons had the kind of lifestyle to which Boris aspired, and the dreariness of the law seemed the way to it. Marrying the daughter of a senior partner might speed up the process, of course, but that had not entered Boris's mind, at least consciously. He had examined his conscience on the matter many times, particularly after the private plane in which Dorothy and her father were flying crashed in the Kansas hills. Grief and anguish gave way to astonishment when the wills were read. Suddenly he was affluent.

He submitted his resignation from the firm, but this was refused. "Give it time," he was advised. "The wounds will heal; life must go on."

Boris had already made preliminary inquiries about buying out the proprietor of an antiquarian bookstore that occupied the ground floor of a downtown building. A year before, he had agonized about making a purchase there; now he was bidding for the whole business.

That had been fifteen years ago, and during that time the rare book business had changed dramatically. Boris Henry Rare Books now had a Web site, which effortlessly brought in both business and opportunities for acquisition. His stock was entered on a national database that consolidated the wares of hundreds of dealers across the country. While Boris still affected condescension toward the computer and the electronic revolution, in his heart of hearts he acknowledged that without such advances his business would be far more onerous than it was. It had become a pleasant, lucrative hobby that made few unwelcome demands on his time.

Clerks came and went, in the manner of clerks, but the principle of stability was Clare Healy. Once Clare would have been classified as a spinster; now she could be regarded as an independent woman. This was, of course, an illusion. She was a willing indentured servant to Boris, bearing the full brunt of the day-to-day details of the business. Where do such women come from? Businesses have them, and universities, too, unmarried women who devote themselves to their jobs so far beyond the call of duty that no salary could begin to compensate them for the work they do.

Had Clare entertained the thought that their relationship might rise above mere business? Boris certainly had. In the early years of her employment, Boris had taken her along on several business trips, and there had been a moment in New Orleans when, flush with wine and the exotic pull of the city, they came very close to becoming lovers. Ironically, it was the wine that saved Boris. Like Dr. Johnson, he found total abstinence less difficult than moderation in drinking. At a heightened moment, sitting in Clara's room, reviewing the exciting day, he had simply fallen asleep. On such contingencies does virtue depend.

He awoke to find that Clara had covered him with a blanket, leaving him in his chair. She was in bed asleep. He crept off to his room, and neither of them ever alluded to how closely they had fluttered to the flame. In the morning, Boris realized that he could never get along without Clara as manager of the business. Even a discreet affair would jeopardize that. From that time on, any overt affection between them was that of brother and sister.

It was Clare who had suggested making Notre Dame books and memorabilia a subset of their offerings. Boris, who had been a wannabe jock in South Bend—this a kind of mask of his wide-ranging intellectual curiosity—had never been personally in the grip of the kind of sentimental loyalty that characterizes so many Notre Dame graduates. Clare's suggestion had taught him how real that continuing interest in their alma mater was to the men and women who had spent four years at Notre Dame, years they invariably claimed were the best of their lives. Under the influence of this sentiment in others, Boris began to acquaint himself with his growing collection of Notre Dame items, and he read Weber's life of John Zahm. Inevitably, books about Notre Dame sports were well represented in his holdings, but it was the history of the university proper that began to interest Boris. He had been a resident of Zahm Hall as an undergraduate but had no curiosity about the Holy Cross priest after whom it was named. The biography opened his eyes.

The writings of Zahm himself were many and various. He had been philosopher and scientist; he began what would develop into the impressive Dante collection at Notre Dame. He had become embroiled in the early disputes over evolution, and he had written about women in science and about women who had inspired great men. But it was Zahm's surprising friendship with Teddy Roosevelt that captured Boris's imagination. Accounts of the journeys the priest and president had taken together intrigued him, particularly those to South America. He remembered Eggs Kittock's account of an expedition in which he had invested. A fantasy formed in his mind, fueled by the character flaw that he had imperfectly concealed from Clare. Boris Henry was a gambler. Casinos near and far drew him as nectar draws the bee. The money he had inherited had financed his book business, and thanks to its success and Clare's stewardship, that business had remained sequestered from his disastrous gambling habit.

An auction in Washington had caught Clare's eye, and when she told Boris why, he went with her. The random lot they were after stressed the printed volumes, some books in which the owner had inscribed his name. John A. Zahm, CSC. Those autographs would have justified buying the lot. They had it shipped back to Kansas City. Some days later, Clare called him and told him to come to the store. There was excitement in her voice. No wonder. At the bottom of the box that contained the books they had gone east for were loose papers and a manuscript tied with a ribbon that disintegrated as Clare attempted to untie it. It was the manuscript of *Up the Orinoco and Down the Magdalena,* the first volume of the two Zahm had written on the conquistadores. Clare looked at him and he looked at Clare. Things like this happened in the book business, but never before to Boris Henry.

"Don't enter it in our catalog," he told her.

"Why not?"

"I think Notre Dame will be interested in buying this."

There was more: Zahm's travel diary on which the books had been based. Boris felt that he had successfully drawn to an inside straight.

The last thing gambling is about is money, however necessary money is to its practice. To gamble is seemingly to take great risks in order to win, but that is only seeming. It is the risk that is the attraction. Winnings when they come never satisfy, save insofar as they provide the basis for further risks. One does not have to be a mathematician to know that eventually every gambler is on the path to penury. While still a young man, Boris had found himself in a financial position that would have permitted him to live a life of leisure. The fact now was that if it were not for his book business, he would be in a very parlous condition indeed. The fantasy he had formed when reading of Zahm's travels south of the border suggested a way out of his difficulties that would leave Boris Henry Rare Books untouched. So it was that he flew off to South Bend.

6 IF THERE WAS A WORM IN THE AP-
ple of Roger Knight's general content-
ment, it was the thought that his brother, Philip, was
sacrificing his life for him. After their parents had died, Phil
had taken responsibility for Roger. He had provided advice
and support during the difficult days before it was established
that Roger was a genius and not an idiot. After graduate
school, Roger's doctorate proved no guarantee of an academic
position; a three-hundred-pound genius was scant competition for the more conventional applicants. He drifted into the
navy, his enlistment the joke of a recruiter about to be discharged. In boot camp, Roger lost weight, but not so much
that he did not float successfully across the pool to qualify as
a swimmer. Agility was never to be his. In the end, he was al-
lowed to while away his days in the base library.

On discharge, he became a partner in Phil's detective
agency. There had been wonderful years when they had
worked out of Rye, New York, accepting only the most chal-
lenging and rewarding of clients. Roger had plenty of time to
develop as a scholar and to enter via the Web into learned ex-
changes with others around the world. It was during a lull in
Rye that he had written his monograph on Baron Corvo, which

had known a surprising success and led to Father Carmody's coming to Rye and offering him the Huneker Chair in Catholic Studies.

"But what would you do?" he asked Phil when his brother urged him to accept.

"Do? I'll come with you."

So he had. The various Notre Dame teams and their home-game schedules enthralled Phil. Or was this something of an act? Did he ever wish that they were back in Rye, considering a potential client's plea for help?

When Phil brought Boris Henry back to the apartment after lunch, Roger was the soul of hospitality. "Kansas City. Phil, remember the work we did for David Joseph?"

"Remind me."

"David Joseph?" Henry said. "He's a client of mine."

"Of yours?"

"My old firm represented him," Henry cried.

They sorted this out, and Boris Henry could not have been any more surprised to learn of the Knight Brothers Agency than Roger was delighted to learn that their guest was a dealer in rare books. David Joseph had been accused of a murder that Roger had demonstrated had never occurred, thus earning Joseph's undying gratitude as well as a handsome fee.

The initial conversation went on like that. How could they seem strangers when they shared so many *tertia quid?* Phil glanced at Henry, but he seemed to understand Roger.

"I wonder what you have in sixteenth- and seventeenth-century Spanish literature." Roger said.

"I'll send you my catalog."

"One of my interests is Lope de Vega. There has never been an edition of his collected works, and I have been gathering them piecemeal."

"Do you have a computer?"

In a trice, Henry and Roger were settled at his computer, and Henry brought up his Web site. There was a listing for the 1614 edition of the *Rimas Sacras,* and Roger bought it on the spot.

Back with Phil, Roger mentioned that he was thinking of doing parallel lives of Cervantes, John of the Cross, and de Vega. "Vega was actually ordained a priest, you know."

Phil broke in. God only knew where all this was leading. "Boris is interested in John Zahm."

"Oh, we've already talked of that, Phil."

If Phil had thought this would get them back to more everyday matters, he must have been disappointed. Boris Henry wanted to know what Roger knew of the South American travels of the Holy Cross priest.

"Only that he made them."

"I have a theory."

Henry's theory seemed made out of whole cloth. He talked of the conquistadores; he spoke of Spanish gold; he reminded Roger of the anxious years during which it had been a daily effort to keep Notre Dame financially afloat. He had convinced himself that Zahm and Teddy Roosevelt had been in search of hidden Spanish gold.

"This is just a guess?" Phil asked, his voice indicating what he thought of such speculation.

"More than a guess. Think of the dome."

Notre Dame's golden dome. Atop the Main Building, which had gone up in 1879, the great dome shone in the daytime sun and, in later years, in nighttime artificial light. It was coated with gold. Boris Henry sat back. Q.E.D.

Even Roger looked disappointed. "There are a number of logical leaps," he said slowly.

But Boris Henry's great middle term was the personality of John Zahm. The man could not have been unaware of the gold that had been taken out of the Spanish colonies, creating a false sense of economic solidity in the old country. Despite all that gold, Spain had foundered and gone under because of external debt to the bankers of Europe. The defeat of the Armada by the English did not help.

"Lope de Vega was there," Henry reminded Roger.

"Do you propose to mount an expedition?"

"Ha. Do you know what that would cost? No, Notre Dame should go after that gold. It could be Zahm's last great gift to the university."

The glint in Boris Henry's eye might have been gold fever. Roger was aware of Phil's reaction to this wild surmise. For all that, he found it fascinating. He was still aglow from the purchase of the *Rimas Sacras*. He and Phil had pursued spoors almost as speculative as this.

"We have to talk with Greg Walsh," Roger said.

"Walsh."

"In the archives. I'll bet he'll come up with something."

"I never bet," Boris Henry said piously.

7 ⟶ WHEN BERNICE ESPERANZA TOLD
people that she worked at Notre Dame
she said no more, letting the name of the university conjure
up in inquiring minds as exalted a position as they wished.
Such hints as she gave created the pardonable impression
that, while not exactly on the faculty, she was centrally engaged in the educational task of the university. If pressed, she
would mention Grace Hall. It was there, in the eatery called
Café de Grasta, that Bernice worked, gliding among the tables, neatening up after diners left. There were slots through
which customers were supposed to slide the remains of their
meals into discreetly concealed trash receptacles, but for the
most part the faculty and administrative staff who had their
lunches there left everything on the table. It was Bernice's
task to clear things away, give the tabletop a few restorative
swipes, and straighten the chairs. She worked from eleven to
three and spent most of that time trying to look like a cus-
tomer rather than one of the help. A graduate student, perhaps.

She told herself that hers was the kind of job that many as-
piring writers had before their moment of recognition came.
She was thirty-four years old and what was now demurely

called a single mom, and the hours of her employment coincided nicely with the time that little Henry spent in day care. Ricardo, her former husband, worked in university maintenance, and the fact that she was on campus five days a week and never ran into him added to her sense that her employment was a disguise.

The divorce had been her idea, arising out of her realization that Ricardo was a clod. She had been twenty-four when they married, and she stuck it out for half a dozen years before she broke the news. Her realization that she was bound to an incompatible mate began when she mentioned enrolling in a creative writing course at IUSB.

Ricardo just stared at her with his mouth hanging open. "What for?"

"For what it says. To learn how to write."

"Write what?"

"Oh, for heaven's sake."

"If you're bored, get a job and bring in some money rather than spend it. What have you ever written?"

Their apartment was cluttered with the romantic novels that made life tolerable for her. Little Henry had been a distraction, of course, but she was careful not to let Ricardo think that she found fussing over a baby the meaning of life. He had an unsettling way of referring to Henry as their *first* child.

Bernice had met Marjorie, another first-time mother, in the hospital.

"What are you going to name him?" Marjorie asked.

"Henry."

Marjorie's brows went up and her eyes widened. "Henry Esperanza?"

Henry had been Bernice's father's name. "My maiden name was Carlyle."

"Mine was Waters." Marjorie paused. "It still is."

"Oh."

That explained why there was no husband in evidence. Given her equivocal status as an unwed mother, Marjorie had a nerve putting on airs. She barely acknowledged it when Bernice introduced her to Ricardo. When he left, Marjorie asked if he was a Mexican.

"Argentine."

"What's that?"

"Is your husband coming?"

"I don't have one."

There was no way to score against Marjorie. She seemed to think that she was striking a blow for independence. She said she might call her daughter Conception. Bernice glowered at her.

"Miss Conception," Marjorie explained.

"Ha ha." It was kind of funny.

Despite everything, they became friends of a sort, and in the subsequent months they got together from time to time. Ricardo didn't like it when Marjorie tried to speak Spanish to him: *Cómo está usted?* When the two women exchanged grievances, Bernice let it go when Marjorie began to refer to Ricardo as Green Card or made a point of how dark Henry was. It was from Marjorie that Bernice learned to think of taking care of Henry as cruel and unusual punishment. She left her daughter with her parents a lot. "I want to resume my career," she had told Bernice in the maternity ward.

"Where do you work?"

She was a receptionist in a realty office and went on about the money she hoped to make selling houses when she passed the exams.

Did she still see her daughter's father? Bernice asked.

"I don't even think of him. What do you plan to do?"

Do? She was a wife and mother. Somehow she knew Marjorie wouldn't take that for an answer. "I may go back to school."

"Where?"

After high school, Bernice had enrolled at IUSB and attended classes fitfully for a few years. The idea was that she would meet someone and get married. She met Ricardo in a sports bar. He was good-looking, no doubt of that, and when he said he worked at Notre Dame she got interested. He was Catholic, so they got married that way; it was all right with Bernice. She believed in God but didn't want to go into any details.

Ricardo didn't make her go to Mass, although Henry was baptized, but it all became an issue when she had had enough. "I don't believe in divorce."

"Ricardo, I'm through."

"Don't you remember what you promised?"

Sometimes Bernice thought that if she didn't have the album of photographs she would never even remember the day she made the mistake of her life. Ricardo dragged her off to a priest who told her that marriage was for life. A life sentence.

That's what it felt like, and she wanted a pardon. Ricardo contested the divorce, but he didn't stand a chance. She had half a mind to let him have Henry.

Marjorie stood by her during the battle. Afterward, she urged Bernice to resume her maiden name.

"I can't do that."

"Why not? It's yours."

"It's the name I intend to write under." She said it on an impulse, to scare away the frightening thought of what she was going to do now. Freedom had looked pretty good until she had it.

"You're going to be an underwriter?"

"Oh ha."

"I'm sorry. Tell me about it."

It was like putting a daydream into words. On the backs of the novels Bernice liked, there were photographs of the authors, and after she finished one Bernice would study the picture and imagine what it would be like to be rich and famous and a novelist. The ambition she described to Marjorie seemed to have been lurking in the back of her mind forever. It was the first time she had ever impressed Marjorie. Later, when she told Marjorie she was at Notre Dame, she tried to make it sound as if she were a student there, but Marjorie just dipped her head and looked at her. Even so, Bernice never told her she worked in the eatery in Grace Hall. If she mentioned her work at all, she referred to "the office." It was Marjorie who encouraged her actually to take the course in creative writing at IUSB. She intended to take it herself. And so they became rivals.

But not for long. Marjorie decided that her talent lay in the direction of descriptive writing. She talked of becoming a reporter. So much for real estate. She took a job answering the phone and accepting ads for a local shoppers' guide. Bernice found it painful to hear her talk about getting out the paper and make odd references to the publishing game, so she told Marjorie she was writing a novel.

"Can I read it?"

"When I'm done."

First she'd have to start it. In the meantime, the course got her going on making notes and keeping a journal and reading with new attention to how a story was told. In her heart of hearts, she was a novelist. That was what drew her to X. Kittock.

That was how she thought of him after noting the name embossed on his briefcase. X the unknown quantity. For a while she played a guessing game about him. He was too old to be a student, even a graduate student, and yet he didn't seem to be faculty. He usually came in about 12:30, and he was still there when the place was empty, everyone else gone. Bernice told herself he hung around because of her. It was only after most people had left that he opened the briefcase and took out a sheaf of papers. When closing time came, it fell to Bernice to tell him they would be locking up. He looked up at her. He looked at the name tag pinned to the flap of her shirt pocket. B. ESPERANZA.

"What's the B for?"

She told him and asked about the X. He told her.

When she left he was waiting in the lobby, and they went

outside, where they sat on a bench. He lit a cigarette. Once he started talking, he couldn't stop. Good Lord, how lonely he seemed. He wouldn't be bad-looking if he took better care of himself.

He shook his head when she asked if he were on the faculty. "I'm here doing research." He exhaled smoke. "I'm a writer."

8 OF LATE FATHER CARMODY HAD felt on the shelf, and there were times when he regretted having moved into Holy Cross House, where he was surrounded by ancients, many content to be old, preparing themselves for their personal last trump, seemingly glad that their active lives were over. Father Carmody was by no means the youngest man in the house, but he was the only one who regarded himself as still active. This conviction required involvement in the events of the day, and as time went by without any indication that the Notre Dame administration still thought of him as a major player, long thoughts came. So it was that the call from the provost was doubly welcome.

"Does the name Boris Henry mean anything to you, Father?"

"Certainly. Kansas City. Class of 1974, unless I'm mistaken."

"You are not mistaken," the provost said, delight in his voice. "And you are just the man I need to consult."

The consultation took place in sybaritic offices in the Main Building. Once the officers of the university had done their work in modest quarters, unassisted by the current armies of supernumeraries occupying rooms that fanned out from the provost's. Ordinarily, Father Carmody would have said something about such conspicuous consumption and the multiplication of associate and assistant provosts and all the rest, but on this occasion he was content to let it go.

They settled on facing sofas, coffee was brought, and the provost got right to the point. "Boris Henry wants the university to set up a John Zahm Center."

"I had no idea he was doing so well."

The provost smiled. "Exactly what I thought at first, but he is not offering to fund the proposed center. As a matter of fact, what he wants to do is sell us some things of Zahm's we do not have."

"Sell!"

"The world has changed, Father."

"But he is an alumnus."

"Be that as it may, I find the idea of such a center intriguing. Of course, the money will have to be found. George Rasp in the foundation suggested you might know of a donor for whom this would be particularly attractive."

"There are many who would find it so, of course."

The provost beamed. The man must have been an undergraduate during Father Carmody's golden years as a power behind the throne.

"What year did you graduate?"

The question startled the provost. "1990. But I'm not a Notre Dame man."

"Good Lord."

"My undergraduate degree is from Princeton."

That the chief academic officer of Notre Dame was a product of such a godless institution as Princeton filled the old priest with dismay. *O tempora, O mores.*

"You will help me on this, won't you, Father?"

"I am always at the service of Notre Dame," Father Carmody said carefully.

From the provost's office, Father Carmody went to Rasp's in the Notre Dame Foundation, the operation that ensured a steady influx of money to the university.

"I come from the provost."

"I know, I know. He called." Rasp had a way of smiling while he talked that Father Carmody found demented. "About the Zahm Center." He spoke as if this entity had already been founded and funded. On the desk before him was a sheet of paper on which he had been making preliminary calculations. "Only a first-class institute will do, and that will require a lot of money."

"Of course, you know who John Zahm was."

"Would you fill me in on that?"

"Are you a Princeton man, too?"

The smile dimmed but then reignited. "Ball State."

There were times when Father Carmody feared that he had lived too long. What would Zahm have made of this kind of interest in his life and work? Boris Henry wanted to sell items to his alma mater; neither the provost nor Rasp seemed to have any idea exactly who Father Zahm had been. In the manner of their kind, though, they recognized a hook for fund-raising.

With resignation, Father Carmody gave a brief sketch of the achievements of John Zahm. Rasp nodded and smiled through the recital.

"I had an intuition," Rasp said when the priest was finished. "After all, if his diary is thought to be worth that much . . ."

"His diary?"

"That is the main item Boris Henry is intent on selling us."

"But we must already have first claim to ownership."

"He bought it at an auction in Washington."

Father Carmody sat back, rendered mute by what this conjured up. God knows what the fate of the items in Holy Cross College in Washington had been. Still, he could scarcely blame that on Princeton men, or alumni of Ball State, for that matter. This perfidy was that of the supposed custodians of the congregation's assets. Of course, some of them were also Princeton graduates.

"Do you have someone in mind, Father?"

"I'll make some calls."

On his way back to Holy Cross House, he detoured past the library, where he consulted the 1974 yearbook. A twenty-two-year-old Boris Henry looked boldly into the camera, all dressed up for his graduation photograph. He figured as well in a photograph dubbed "the Three Musketeers." Boris Henry, Xavier Kittock, and Paul Lohman. It all came back to him now. Three rowdies if there ever were, roommates in Zahm. Which one had climbed the scaffolding surrounding the dome when it was being regilded and descended with a souvenir to the cheers of the onlookers? Despite himself, the memory elicted a smile.

All that had been long ago Kittock had gone through Notre Dame on an ROTC scholarship and ended in the navy. Henry had gone into the law in Kansas City. Lohman, the least likely member of the trio, a dean's list student for four years, had narrowly missed being named valedictorian of his class. Several patents on devices used in communication satellites had made him enormously rich. Funding the John Zahm Center would be well within the range of his generosity, a mere bagatelle. Father Carmody put through a call to Boston.

SCHOLARLY INTERESTS EBB AND flow, obeying some astral influence beyond the ken of man. That is how Greg Walsh would have archly put it if his speech impediment had not reduced him to the status of a Trappist. Oddly enough, his tongue was loosened with Roger Knight, and whenever the great dirigible of a man squeezed through the entrance to the university archives, Greg enjoyed a holiday from his handicap. Roger had sent an e-mail telling Greg he was coming over. It was midafternoon in the archives. It might have been siesta time in some Mediterranean village. Not even Xavier Kittock was on the premises.

Greg went into the workroom, where gray archival boxes stood in a neat row on the table. It was a concession to Kittock to keep them in this room rather than return them to storage each day. Tapping the tops of the boxes with his fingers, Greg sighed. Zahm. Suddenly everyone was interested in Zahm. Roger's e-mail had contained a line or two about Boris Henry. A Google search on Henry featured his rare book business. The Notre Dame database turned up some interesting items. While he was at it, Greg ran a search on Kittock. Well, now he had an idea of Boris Henry's age. He and Kittock had been classmates at Notre Dame, and sure enough, they had both lived in Zahm Hall. But Greg could hardly make his complaint to Roger. After all, the Huneker Professor of Catholic Studies was himself lecturing on Father John Zahm this semester.

"Partly in response to a suggestion by Father Carmody," Roger had explained, "but mostly because he seems to have been the most interesting faculty member of his generation."

Of course, Greg knew the Zahm holdings in the archives, but then he knew the whole vast potpourri crammed into these rooms on the sixth floor of Hesburgh Library like the back of his hand.

The entrance opened, setting off a bell, and through the glass of the workroom Greg watched Roger squeeze through the door, wearing the deferential smile that came and went when he was reminded of his girth. Greg went out to greet him. Although their talking would disturb no one, Greg took him into the workroom and closed the door.

"Busy day?"

"As you see."

"So you have the place all to yourself." Roger had eased himself into a chair, effectively making it disappear. His hand went out to the row of archival boxes on the table. He turned one toward himself. "Zahm?"

"Who else?"

"Did you get these out for me?"

Greg found it a pleasant thought that he would know without being told what the purpose of Roger's visit was. He explained about Xavier Kittock. "He was a classmate of your Boris Henry."

"What is his interest in Zahm?" Roger asked.

"He is very secretive. That, of course, makes me curious."

"And?"

Greg leaned toward Roger. "He is writing a life of Zahm for teenagers."

Again the bell, and Kittock hurried into the archives. He came to a halt when he saw that the workroom was occupied.

Greg stood and went out to reassure Kittock. "We just stepped in there to talk. Come, I want you to meet someone." In his haste he forgot to stammer.

Kittock hesitated. He was clearly flustered. He hugged his briefcase to his chest. He still hugged it, as if for protection, when they went into the workroom, where Greg introduced him to Roger Knight.

Kittock freed one hand and extended it to the still-seated Roger. "Of course I've heard of you."

"Of course?"

"My niece is in your class. Rebecca Nobile."

"A very intelligent young lady. And I don't refer to her choice of professors." Roger's chuckle set off a seismic movement in his enormous body that seemed to descend from his chins, ripple across his vast chest, and continue like a landslide to his surprisingly small feet, which were enclosed in sandals. The toes of them rose and fell rhythmically. "Greg tells me you are interested in Father Zahm."

Kittock glanced at Greg. "In a small way."

Greg tried to voice his mot about the ebb and flow of scholarly interests, but his tongue would not oblige. Even the secretive Kittock stilled his voice.

"I understand Boris Henry was your classmate," Roger said, his voice suggesting that he had a surprise in store for Kittock.

The effect was electric. Kittock sprang back from the seated professor and got his hand on the knob of the door. Again he pressed his briefcase to his chest. "Why do you mention him?"

"Because of his interest in Father Zahm. I just left him."

"He's already here!" Kittock swung on Greg, as if he were the cause of his confusion. "I won't be working this afternoon. You can put those boxes away." He bobbed at Roger, left the workroom, and a moment later was out of the archives. Roger looked at Greg. The archivist shrugged.

"I wonder if Boris Henry will react in the same way when I tell him Kittock has been doing research on Father Zahm?" Greg speculated.

Soon Kittock's odd behavior was forgotten, and they turned to the object of Roger's visit.

"I want to see everything on Zahm's South American trips. With and without Teddy Roosevelt."

Greg pulled one of the boxes on the worktable from the row. "You can start with this."

"Is that Kittock's interest?"

"I told you. He's all over the lot. The evolution controversy, the trips out west to recruit students, Dante, stories about him in the *Scholastic*. You name it."

Roger was not likely to criticize a scattergun approach to a subject. He nodded as if in approval of Kittock's method, or lack of it. He was already examining the contents of the box Greg had indicated. The archivist went in search of more materials. An hour later, Roger was so immersed that Greg felt he was interrupting when he put the photocopy of the story in the *Observer* before Roger. For a moment, he wondered if Roger had noticed, but then Roger picked it up and read, a smile forming on his face.

The story was headlined GOLD FEVER and recounted the regilding of the dome on the Main Building. Greg had underlined the paragraphs that described the ascent of the scaffolding by Boris Henry. There was a photograph of him taken when he came down, holding a golden chip.

10 JOSH DALEY RAN EVERY OTHER day, at least five miles, sometimes ten, depending on whether or not he confined himself to the campus roads and the paths around the lakes. This was the safer course. Running north on the county road to the Michigan line added the hazard of traffic to the welcome punishment of fatigue. On the day after he had finally met Rebecca he ran fifteen miles, on campus and off, and he returned to the Joyce Center soaked with perspiration. The exercise seemed a metaphor of his life. He was a long distance runner, and he hoped he had embarked on a long run with Rebecca.

If he had looked forward to Continental epistemology before talking with Rebecca, now the class seemed the main purpose of his life. Although he feared it would make Tenet even less intelligible, Josh plunked down beside Rebecca and got a smile for his pains. There were three minutes before the lecture began.

"So you're a philosophy major," he said to Rebecca.

"Why aren't you?"

"I'll tell you a secret. If Tenet lectured in German it would make as much sense to me."

"Come on."

"I mean it."

"What is your major?"

"Don't laugh."

"Tell me."

He told her. She laughed.

"It would help if you explained the course to me."

She saw that he was serious. "On one condition."

"Name it."

"That you come to Professor Knight's class tomorrow."

He had already agreed to do this. Had she forgotten? "It's a deal." It was a date, too, sort of.

Tenet was at the podium shuffling his papers. The clock ticked, and he began, addressing Josh as if he had identified the ideal student. Josh busied himself with his notebook rather than let Tenet see how lost he was. He wrote rapidly what he could remember of the Gettysburg Address. Beside him, Rebecca paused between quick entries in her notebook. From time to time she nodded in agreement with Tenet. The topic was the Leibnitzian monad. It sounded like a railroad. Without windows. Nothing really acted on anything else; it just appeared that way because of preestablished harmony. Philosophy seemed a lot like science fiction.

Afterward, when they were walking across campus, he told her that he ran.

"From what?"

"Just run. You know."

"Jogging?"

"Sort of."

"That seems such a waste of time."

If she had asked him to, he would have sworn off running then and there. Instead she said, "Maybe I should try it."

"How about later?"

"You're serious."

He was. It wasn't his day to run, but he was serious. He didn't want to leave her at her dorm and then wait for Tenet's next class. That would be next week.

An hour later, they were running together on the lake path. Josh kept it slow. She made it around the first lake and then cried, "Help." They sat on a bench and were soon surrounded by ducks.

"How often do you do this?"

"Every other day."

"You're not even breathing hard."

"I'm used to it."

"I didn't realize how out of shape I am." She paused and laughed.

"What?"

"Wait till you see Roger Knight."

He saw him the next day. Knight looked like he could float over the stadium on game days, a real blimp. Rebecca took him up to the huge professor and said that Josh wanted to sit in. "He lives in Zahm Hall." "Ah."

"You can ask him about the Treaty of Westphalia."

She had to explain that. Knight seemed amused. By the look of him, Josh would have expected him to be as disorganized as Tenet, but then he began talking—and that's what it was, talking, not lecturing. Even better, Josh had no trouble following.

Knight was talking about the summer lecture circuits Zahm used to take part in. "Anyone ever heard of chautauquas?"

"An Indian tribe?" It was a guess from the back of the room.

Knight laughed. Josh raised his hand and explained what the chautauqua circuit was. Rebecca beamed at him.

Knight took up where Josh left off. Then he was on to Zahm's interest in evolution and the trouble it had gotten him into. He quoted the great man to the effect that we now— Zahm's "now," that is—knew the earth was at least ten thousand years old. "You have to remember how long ago this was. Even so, it sounded like a dangerous position to many."

The period went by like a breeze, and Josh was wishing he had known about this course when he signed up for Continental epistemology. When the time was up, no one wanted to leave, so it went on for another half hour informally. Finally, Knight got to his feet, everyone pulling for him. He made it.

They all escorted him out to his golf cart. Clambering in, he announced, "I'm having an open house Saturday afternoon. You're all invited." Then he was off, scattering pedestrians as he zoomed along the walk.

Rebecca said, "You have to come."

"You're going?"

"Of course. It's better than a class."

The class had met in Brownson Hall, behind Sacred Heart. Once it had been a convent; now it had been remodeled to contain a few classrooms and faculty offices, including Knight's. They were passing Washington Hall when someone called Rebecca's name. A middle-aged guy. She ran up to him and gave him a hug, and then she was introducing Josh to her Uncle X.

"How's the research going?" Rebecca asked.

"Slowly."

She reached out and patted her uncle's tummy. "Don't let yourself go."

He backed away from her, embarrassed. "It comes with age."

"Age! You're younger than Mom."

Although he had initiated the encounter, Kittock seemed eager to leave them. Rebecca stopped babbling about the class they were coming from and let him go with the suggestion that they get together soon for dinner at Papa Vino's. He nodded and then turned and marched away, out of place among the young.

"The black sheep," Rebecca whispered.

"How so?"

"I'll tell you sometime."

That was okay with Josh. He preferred having her bright-eyed curiosity directed at himself.

11 RICARDO ESPERANZA — BERNICE always insisted on calling him Ricardo— had emigrated from Argentina, where he might have led another sort of life, one of bourgeois poverty. His father had taught courses at several universities in Buenos Aires and spent his days in a private institute funded by CONICET, the rough Argentine equivalent of the National Endowment for the Humanities. None of this brought in enough money for a family of five children, and the Argentine economy offered little basis for future hope for those children. Ricardo had attended the Catholic University of Buenos Aires, which offered little more than a passport to the kind of hand-to-mouth existence his father could provide. For all that, his memories of his homeland were pleasant. He had spent long evenings strolling the Via Florida, flirting with girls. It was a matter of honor as well as habit to stay up half the night. Everyone did. When he went to the opera and emerged at midnight, all the restaurants were going full blast and the night was young. After Bernice divorced him, he thought of returning, but how could he explain to his family what had happened to his marriage? He couldn't explain it to himself.

Of course, he had lied about his job; he just told them he

was employed by the University of Notre Dame. He earned more on the maintenance crew than his father had ever earned as a professor of classics. The drop in social status had spelled economic security. Marrying Bernice had been another downward step, so it wounded him the more that she had left him. During his life with Bernice, he had more or less concealed his origins, determined to dwell on her level. Now that he was alone, he had renewed his earlier interests: the classics his father had taught him even before he went to school; music. He might have been rinsing his soul of the house filled with gaudy paperbacks and the constant thunder of rock. Still, he missed Bernice, and little Henry, more than he would have admitted. His visits on the days he was permitted time with his son were seasons in hell.

Now Bernice was working on campus! He had learned this from Marjorie when he ran into her at the supermarket.

"I suppose you got her the job?"

Well, there were women in maintenance, but it was pretty hard to think of Bernice as one of them.

"Notre Dame is the biggest local employer."

"Maybe I'll apply."

Marjorie was the kind of American woman he had imagined before he came here. One thing he had to give Bernice, she let him make the first move. When he left Marjorie he felt that he was escaping. Even if she had been a lot better looking, Ricardo still considered himself to be married to Bernice.

Bernice. What the hell was she doing at Notre Dame? Working as a waitress, it turned out. He had sat in his pickup in the parking lot of Grace and watched her come to work.

60

Throughout that day, he went back, unable to believe it. He was more embarrassed about her new job than she was. When he had taunted her about getting a job, he hadn't meant it. His mother had never worked, no matter how tight things were. It was unmanly to let your wife work. A husband was supposed to support his wife and children, and in this country he could, so why the hell were all these women working?

Then one day he saw her sitting at an outside table with an older man. Bernice was all over the guy. She must have taken lessons from Marjorie. He tried to tell himself it was nothing, just some professor she wanted to tell about all her crazy ambitions. Sure. But he found out who the guy was.

Xavier Kittock. Like Xavier Cugat, from American movies he had seen in Buenos Aires.

The next day, Ricardo hopped out of his pickup and confronted the guy on a campus walk.

"I am Ricardo Esperanza."

"Do I know you?"

"Bernice is my wife."

He just nodded.

"You know Bernice?" Ricardo persisted.

"The girl who works in Grace."

"Keep away from her. She's my wife."

He stepped closer, and the man danced away. Several people stopped, wondering what the maintenance guy was up to.

"Just remember," Ricardo growled, and went back to his pickup.

12 ➤ "KITTOCK? EGGS KITTOCK?" BORIS
Henry reacted to the mention of the man
currently doing research in the archives with a mixture of annoyance and amusement. "We were roommates here. There
were three of us together. Eggs, Paul Lohmam, and myself."
For a moment, Greg feared that Boris was going to drift into
reminiscing about his student days, always a threat where
alumni are concerned. "What the devil is Eggs Kittock doing
in the archives?"

Greg assumed a pious look. It was not for him to divulge
one person's research to another. This moral high ground had
the added advantage of making his silence seem virtuous.

"How often does he come?"

"Often."

Boris was led to the glassed-in workroom, and his attention
was drawn immediately to the row of boxes on the table. He
hardly glanced at them before asking why they were already
out. "This is the stuff I wanted to look at. The correspon-
dence."

"There's more. It's catalogued by year."

"Has Kittock been looking at this stuff?"

"Yes."

With an effort, Henry let it go. There was no point in letting the archivist see how upset he was. But Eggs Kittock, for the love of God! Research? The workroom door closed after Walsh, and Henry opened the flip top of the first box, but then he just sat there. Someone was playing a trick on him. Someone had somehow got wind of his interest in Zahm, particularly the Latin American travels, and was using it to tweak him. Then he remembered. Of course. Eggs had come through Kansas City some months ago, and after a sumptuous dinner they sat up half the night talking. What hadn't they talked about? Like an idiot, he must have said enough about Zahm for Eggs to put two and two together, though how he managed to remember anything after all they had drunk was a wonder. He looked awful when Boris introduced him to Clare late the following morning. Clare, the wonder woman, said she immediately recognized Eggs from the photograph in Boris's office of the three roommates in their senior year. More important, she mixed him a bromo and restored him to more or less normal condition.

"What a night," he moaned.

"I don't want to hear about it."

Clare sounded almost flirty, and Boris looked at her in surprise.

Maybe she thought she could jolly visiting firemen without complications. For a fleeting moment, Boris recalled their own near thing. He wouldn't say he was jealous, but, hey, who was the boss here anyway?

"You want a bromo, too?" Clare asked him.

"What for?" At the moment, he would have heatedly denied feeling queasy. Drinking too much almost seemed meritorious, since he never felt the impulse to gamble then. The casinos demanded an absolutely clear head.

Of course, he and Eggs would have talked of Paul. Their own lives, his and Paul's, seemed obscenely successful compared with poor Eggs's. On the basis of some patents used in communication satellites, Paul had made his pile and now had all the time in the world to devote himself to reading and music.

"You should have married," Boris had said to Eggs.

"It's too late for that," He glanced at Clare when he said it, though.

"Oh, come on."

"Or I'm too selfish. You're in no rush to escape the single state, I notice."

"There's plenty of time."

"Clare is a very beautiful woman," Eggs said later.

"Is she? I don't even notice anymore."

So that was a possibility, Boris thought as he sat in the workroom of the archives at Notre Dame. It would be like Eggs to plan an elaborate leg pull, but would old Paul have gone along with it? Then again, the three of them had played two-on-one jokes as undergraduates. Lots of fun, except when you were the one on the receiving end.

What he couldn't comprehend was the thought of Eggs Kittock sitting here in the archives doing research, and on Zahm. It made no sense. His impression was that Eggs spent most of his time on the golf course down in Sarasota, where he had settled. Eggs had been a mediocre student and would have floundered after graduation if he hadn't gone into the service. He had been a twenty-year man in the navy, maybe a few years more. That had been his element. He had been through a good share of the hell of recent years and had survived to claim his pension. Then he had embarked on a number of quixotic schemes. The sunken treasure expedition! Once Boris remembered that, Eggs working in the archives no longer seemed a joke.

The Three Musketeers had kept in touch by way of e-mail since Eggs got out of the navy, but the only time they had all gotten together was at a class reunion three years ago. It had been wonderful. Eggs had seemed bemused by the fact that Boris was in the rare books business.

"Does it pay?"

Boris made a noncommital noise. Both Eggs and Paul knew he had come into a fortune when he lost his wife and father-in-law in that plane crash. Maybe they thought dealing in rare books was just a hobby. At the time of the reunion, Boris had not yet become fascinated with John Zahm, but he had mentioned the lucrative Notre Dame facet of his business. Eggs's visit to Kansas City had come after that, and Boris was suddenly sure he had told Eggs of the Zahm diary. Of course, anyone who got interested in Zahm could have come up with the same hunch Boris had, but given Eggs's interest in buried treasure it seemed a certainty that he had. The fact was that no one during all the years since Zahm died had put two and two together. But Eggs, for crying out loud. Did the guy read anything? Now that he thought of it, Boris remembered Eggs asking if there was a copy of Richard Sullivan's book on Notre Dame among his holdings.

"Check the Web site. I'm sure we have it."

"I've been reading Ed Fisher and Tom Stritch."

Two professors who had published their memoirs, which concentrated on Notre Dame. Suddenly, it no longer seemed implausible that Eggs had hit on the same idea Boris had. His hand went out to the archival box, filled with Zahm letters. They were on the table because Eggs had asked for them.

He was no longer in a mood to pursue the spoor that had brought him back to campus. First, he had to talk with Eggs.

(13) ----→ SEVEN STUDENTS SHOWED UP ON
Saturday afternoon at the Knights' apart-
ment, where Roger treated them to huge bowls of popcorn and
the drink of their choice. Most of them followed his example
and had soft drinks, but there was Phil's beer for those who
wanted it. It was when he was talking with Rebecca that
Roger learned that her uncle was on campus, working in the
archives. Greg had mentioned Xavier Kittock, the man who
was looking through Zahm materials, but it was a surprise to
learn he was Rebecca's uncle.

"It must run in the family," he said.

"What?"

Roger shrugged. "Well, after all, your father is a fan of Lope
de Vega."

She laughed. "Uncle X is not at all like my father. He's my
mother's brother. He's not like her, either."

"X?"

"For Xavier. He spent most of his life in the navy."

"I'm a navy man myself."

She sat back, as if to gain sufficient distance to take him all
in. Her look was one of disbelief, so he told her of his igno-
minious naval career.

"You actually wore one of those uniforms?"

"There was less of me then. Not much less, but enough."

"Well, Uncle X was made for the navy. In the family, he is something of a black sheep. Before and after the navy, that is. He was discharged with a chest full of medals."

"And what does he do now?"

"Golfs. He does read. And a few years ago he was part of a treasure hunting expedition. Basically, he's retired. He's younger than my mother, and already he's retired. My dad can't understand how he can spend all his time doing nothing."

"Golf isn't nothing."

"Don't tell me you golf, too?"

It was Roger's turn to laugh. "I leave that to my brother, Phil."

"Is he retired?"

"I don't think he would put it that way."

"What does he do?"

"He's a private detective."

"I don't believe it."

"It's true." Roger decided against telling her that he himself had a private investigator's licence.

"He and Uncle X should get together."

"They could golf."

"Would you mind if I suggested it?"

Roger hesitated. He didn't want to commit Phil, and he could imagine his brother's reaction to the suggestion that he golf with a man who spent his days in the university archives. Of course, there was the naval career to balance that.

"Why don't you ask Phil?" he suggested. "But first, tell me more about your father."

He had been a successful pathologist in Fort Worth, Rebecca said, a specialty that left him time for the pursuits that increasingly interested him. The move to Texas had prompted him to learn Spanish, and that had led to an interest in Spanish literature. Hence Lope de Vega.

"I'd like to meet him."

"And he wants to meet you. Next time he visits I'll set it up. Meanwhile, I want to talk to your brother." Off she went to Phil, who was in the den watching television, staying out of the way of Roger's class.

"Thanks for letting me come." It was Josh Daley.

"Have some more popcorn."

Josh had some more popcorn as he explained why he had shown up for Roger's class.

"What's your major?"

"History."

"What period?"

"Modern European."

"How modern?"

"Post-Reformation and into the eighteenth century."

"Spain?"

"Some. Why do you ask?"

"Spanish literature is Rebecca's father's passion. The golden age, one of the most fascinating of all, with St. Teresa of Avila and St. John of the Cross as well as Cervantes and Lope de Vega."

"That's Rebecca's middle name."

"Now you know why."

Was Roger actually suggesting that the way to Rebecca's heart was via her father's interest in Spanish literature? When Josh thought of it that way, it sounded pretty silly. Still, being polite never hurt.

"Thanks for the tip," he said.

14 XAVIER KITTOCK HAD FOUND HIS return to campus everything that he had expected. The weather was contrast enough to Florida's to give zest to life. He sprang out of bed in the morning and into the shower as if he were on some demanding schedule, and he loved it. Ever since getting out of the navy, he had been fulfilling the dream of indolence that carries one through the working years. When it comes, though, it swiftly loses its charms. The thing about a vacation is that it's temporary, a furlough; retirement just goes on and on. Who would have thought that you could get tired of golf? The expedition to find buried treasure seemed to bring him back to active duty, and it led to other things. Now, back at Notre Dame, he had a routine. His room was only a notch above a student room; there were all kinds of places to pick up breakfast. At 11:30, he went to Mass in Sacred Heart Basilica, surprised at how easily piety returned in this setting. Then there were the long hours in the archives.

Suddenly this idyll had been disturbed. First, there had been Bernice, the girl in the eatery at Grace, where he often went for a long lunch after a morning in the archives. He felt like an ass when he remembered telling her he was a writer.

That had led to her telling him of her ambitions. Hers seemed a commentary on his own imaginary aspirations. It was pretty obvious that Bernice wanted to be an author, but it was unclear whether she could be a writer. Was he any better? They both wanted the title without the effort. This sense of similarity made him more sympathetic to her rather than less. Then he had been publicly confronted by her husband!

Lying on his bed, shoes kicked off, hands behind his head, he sought on the ceiling the memory of that encounter. His first impulse was to tell the man that he had it all wrong—Bernice was so much younger, the accusation was ridiculous—but how could he justify himself with people slowing down and listening in as the man all but shouted his accusation on a campus walk? Then he was gone, and Kittock hurried away to his room and the replaying of the humiliating episode. One thing was sure, he would never return to the eatery in Grace. If he got serious about any woman at his age it would be Clare Healy.

Now Boris Henry was looking for him. Greg Walsh had phoned Kittock and managed to get out that message with some effort. Kittock thanked him and hung up and then wondered why the archivist felt he should warn him about Boris. Of course, it was Zahm. Kittock thought of Boris seeing that row of boxes on the table in the workroom of the archives. Naturally he would think that Kittock was poaching on his territory.

Well, he was. At the reunion, on a walk around the lakes, Paul Lohman had gone on and on about the transformation in their old friend, from lawyer to leading rare book dealer. "What he doesn't know," Paul said in admiration. "He sounds like a professor with a dozen specialities. Do you know *The Great Gatsby?*"

"The novel?"

"Boris quoted from it. 'I was that narrowest of specialists, the well-rounded man.'"

"What's that mean?"

"Ask Boris. He carries a lot of Notre Dame stuff. He says it sells like candy. You know the hall we lived in, Zahm? Named after a priest, John Zahm. He's become a big interest of Boris's."

That was all, at least about Boris. He and Paul played nine holes, and Eggs took it easy on his old roommate. His own handicap was down to four, but he was almost ashamed of that, listening to Boris Henry's exciting life. Then had come the visit to Kansas City and the exciting news about Zahm's travel diary. So he got hold of Weber's biography of Zahm, and the next thing he knew he was sitting in the archives at Notre Dame asking the archivist to bring him stuff on Zahm. Well, it was one thing to fool a girl who worked in Grace. Boris wouldn't need two minutes to see how little Eggs Kittock had learned during his weeks in the archives.

He called the Morris Inn and asked for the room of Boris Henry. He was registered, but Kittock didn't leave a message. Better to just go over there and meet him when he came in.

Half an hour later, as Kittock entered the Morris Inn lobby, a girl rose from a chair and hurried up to him. Good God, Bernice.

"I thought you would be staying here," she said.

"But I'm not."

She waved it away as an irrelevancy. "Did my husband threaten you?"

Eggs looked wildly around, but no one seemed to be paying attention. A good thing. Bernice was clinging to his arm and looking up into his face with more excitement than anger.

"I could kill him," she said.

He took her outside, and they sat at a table where they wouldn't be visible from the dining room. Eggs tried to laugh away her anger with her husband, but it became clear that she was enjoying this.

"I don't know how he found out about you," Bernice said.

"There's nothing to find out."

"Try to convince him of that."

"I don't think so." What he was thinking was that it was time he got the hell back to Florida, teed up a ball, and went back to being Eggs Kittock. He would leave Zahm to Boris.

"I can't tell you how bad I feel."

"Look, I am a middle-aged man. This is ridiculous." She wasn't that much older than Rebecca. Well, anyway, she was one helluva lot younger than he was. Nor was she anyone men would fight over—past any prettiness she had once known, and not managing too well now that she was older. Her thin face was long; her mousy hair responded to the slightest breeze. The big staring eyes were hungry for something she was unlikely to find. Involuntarily, he compared her with the sophisticated and mature Clare Healy. It was one thing to chat with the girl where she worked, but now she had come to the Morris Inn on the assumption that he was staying here and had sat in the lobby until he showed up. Hadn't she even checked at the desk?

"Did you go to the archives?"

"I had to tell you how upset I am."

"Well, I appreciate that." He stood. "I hope you work things out with your husband."

"We're divorced."

"I'm sorry."

"Why?"

"Okay, I'm not sorry."

She gave him a slow, sly smile. Good God. She was still seated in her chair when the doors from the lobby opened and Rebecca came out.

"Uncle X," she cried. Then she noticed Bernice. Her eyes went back and forth from her uncle to the girl. "Oh. Sorry. I saw you from the lobby and. . . ."

Bernice was standing. Rebecca looked as if she expected Eggs to introduce her to the girl. Not on your life. He took his niece's arm and went with her into the lobby.

"Who was that?" Rebecca whispered.

"Darned if I know. She was there when I stepped outside."

"Better be careful. She looks as if she'd like to have you for lunch."

15 BORIS HENRY LOPED ACROSS THE lobby of the Morris Inn and stopped.

"Eggs!"

Kittock actually jumped at the sound of his name, but the girl with him smiled receptively. Boris put his hands on Eggs's shoulders. "You old pirate. How are you?"

"This is my niece, Rebecca."

"Well, that's a relief. I thought you were going through a midlife crisis."

"I'm looking forward to it."

"Let's all have a drink."

"Not me," Rebecca cried. "I saw Uncle X on his way here and have been trying to catch up to him." She turned to Eggs. "Dad is coming on a visit."

"Your mother, too?"

"Just Dad." She leaned toward Eggs and kissed him. "Call me." Off she went.

As Kittock and Boris headed for the bar, Bernice came in from the patio. "Oh," she said. "I wasn't sure you were coming back." She tipped back her head so she could look up at Boris.

"So who have we here?" Boris chortled.

"Bernice. Bernice Esperanza." She thrust a hand at Boris,

and he enclosed it in both of his. He looked at Eggs, waiting for him to do the honors.

"This is my classmate, Boris Henry."

"Henry! That's my son's name."

"Reason enough to buy you a drink. Will you join us?" Boris asked.

That not all prayers are answered was proved once more to Kittock when she accepted with a giggle. She went into the bar on Boris's arm, and Eggs followed.

There are stretches of time so unwelcome that every moment of their duration is burnt into memory. When they were settled at a table—a glass of white wine in front of the bedazzled Bernice, Boris with a scotch and water, and Eggs settling for a Miller Lite as if to punish his classmate with his moderation—Eggs felt both spectator at and participant in a farce. Boris was enjoying this too much, quizzing Bernice, feigning fascination with her answers.

"You're employed at Notre Dame?"

"Xavier can tell you all about it."

"But will he?" Boris asked, his brows actually dancing.

"There is nothing to hide."

"Eggs always was the brazen sort."

"Eggs?"

"That's what we call him. Eggs for X."

"Oh, that's funny."

Incredibly, Boris elicited from her her hopes of becoming a writer. "It's what Eggs and I have in common," she said.

"Of course." Boris glanced at Eggs, who got his glass to his mouth. "Who are your favorite authors?"

"Oh, you wouldn't have heard of them."

"Try me."

"Boris is in the book business," Eggs said.

"A publisher!"

"No, no. Merely a dealer. Rare books mainly."

"Oh, that's fascinating."

"But tell me how you two met."

"You tell him," Bernice urged, but Eggs waved his hand, giving her the floor. "We have lunch in the same place on campus," she said.

Dante was wrong in the punishments he selected for the souls in Purgatory. What could be more punitive than the situation Kittock found himself in? Bernice made their meeting at the eatery in Grace seem like an assignation.

"Of course, it's all quite innocent." She widened her eyes. "No matter what my husband thinks."

"Your husband?"

"Actually we're divorced, but try to get him to realize that. He threatened Eggs."

"Physically?"

"You'd have to know Ricardo to understand. He's an Argentine. Very macho."

"And jealous, it would seem."

"Isn't that silly?"

"Oh, I don't know."

By the slow movement of the setting sun she could not have remained with them for twenty minutes, but for Eggs the torture seemed prolonged for eons.

Suddenly, in a flurry, she pushed back her chair. "What time is it?"

Boris told her.

She gave a little squeaking cry and scrambled to her feet. "Henry," she explained. She stood for a moment, unsuccessfully seeking the right words, and then, with a little bow at each of them, turned and headed for the door. A man was waiting for her. Dear God, it was her husband.

"It seems she had a double date," Boris said.

Silhouetted in the doorway, one hand gripping Bernice's arm, Ricardo peered into the ill-lit bar. Eggs actually shrank in his chair. Then they were gone.

"So you're here doing research?" Boris said with a chuckle.

"She's a waitress in the restaurant in Grace."

"Now, don't apologize."

Eggs ordered a Manhattan, pushing away his undrunk beer. He felt the need for strong drink. Boris continued to tease him for a time and then lost interest.

"Do you know why I'm here?" Boris asked.

"Tell me."

"Not to jolly waitresses." He grew serious. "I am here to persuade the university to open a John Zahm Center."

After Boris rapidly outlined his plan, Eggs had to admit it was a great idea. "And you're going to finance it?"

Boris sat back, seemed about to say something, then hesitated. Then, "Not entirely."

"Just donating the travel diary would amount to so much. Your tax man would be delighted."

"Of course, the diary belongs at Notre Dame."

"Greg Walsh got the idea you intended to sell it to the university."

"Strange fellow. Now, what's this about you being a writer?"

"Do you believe everything a waitress tells you?"

"Eggs, the girl is nuts about you."

"Then why was she fawning over you?"

"To make you jealous. What's this about her husband?"

"What she said. He threatened me."

"What a romantic figure you've become."

"When are you going to let me see Zahm's travel diary?"

"I'm afraid you might organize an expedition and go in search of El Dorado."

"What's that got to do with the diary?"

"Guess."

"Where are you staying?"

"Right here."

"Well, I'm in the Jamison Inn. I'd better get going."

"Not interested in dinner?"

"Not tonight."

They rose and shook hands, and as Eggs left the bar Boris called after him. "Watch out for husbands."

LATE THAT AFTERNOON, BORIS Henry stepped out of the workroom at the archives and beckoned Greg Walsh to come in. When the archivist entered, Boris shut the door and went to the table, where he pushed a box toward Greg. "Tell me what you make of that."

"The letters of Father Zahm?"

"Take a good look."

Greg sat and began to leaf through the identifying tabs in the box while Boris stood in an expectant attitude. Greg looked up. "What am I looking for?"

"Let me put it this way. If you were looking for letters from 1914 and 1915, you wouldn't find them."

Greg again went through the contents of the box, more carefully now. When he was finished, he turned to a computer and brought up the archives Web site. Boris could see that he was checking the contents of the box as recorded there. After several minutes, he turned and once more went through the actual box. Then he sat back.

"They're not here."

"So I found. And Kittock was the last one to deal with the contents of that box, right?"

"You think he took them?"

"Well, they're not there. Of course, there may be an innocent explanation."

It was clear that Greg Walsh could not think of one. There was now a deep frown on the archivist's face. The materials in the archives represented a sacred trust, and he was unlikely to regard missing materials as a routine matter.

"Could he have walked away with them?" Boris asked.

Greg was checking the drawers of the worktable. When they yielded nothing, he made a careful search of the workroom. Finally, he slumped once more in a chair and put his face in his hands and groaned. "Why would he take them?"

Boris was about to say that Kittock was intent on sabotaging his own effort, but he had not told Walsh, as he had Roger Knight, of his wild hunch. However wild, it had come to seem almost established fact. "I have a suggestion," he said instead.

"What?"

"Let's tell Roger Knight about this."

Walsh was immediately on his feet, nodding. "Good idea."

Walsh called the Knight apartment before they left the archives. Listening, Boris was surprised at the fluency with which Walsh told Roger that he had to see him immediately. Something very odd had happened.

"Boris Henry will be coming with me," Walsh said before hanging up.

Walsh locked the door of the archives and then glanced at Boris. Such precautions seemed a little late.

"Does Kittock have a key to that door?" Boris asked.

"Of course not."

No one could use materials from the archives unless Greg or one of the other archivists was on the premises. It wasn't stated that this amounted to keeping an eye on anyone working with archival materials, but that, of course, is what the reason for the rule must originally have been.

At the Knight apartment, they were greeted by Roger. The expression on Greg Walsh's face was soon matched by concern on the massive countenance of the Huneker Professor of Catholic Studies.

"Some Zahm letters are missing from the archives," Walsh announced.

"The very ones I came here to see," Boris added.

"Well, well. Do you have a suspect?"

Boris let Greg make the accusation. "I told you about Kittock," he said. "But you hadn't met him."

"No, I hadn't." Roger paused. "I'll put on coffee."

He made a production of it, and until he was done and the coffee ready the conversation was suspended. Boris had the idea that Roger Knight had wanted this time to ponder what he had been told. When they all had their coffee, they sat in Roger's study. The professor took the specially built swivel chair in which he could move easily from computer to desk to bookshelves.

"From the beginning," he suggested.

The beginning Greg Walsh chose was two weeks before when X. Kittock had first shown up at the archives. As an alumnus, he was, of course, welcome, and there was no need for formal permission to use the archives. Ever since, for half of each day, he had made use of the workroom, from time to time asking for new materials and surrendering those he had already examined.

"He always asked for Zahm materials?"

Greg thought. "Not always. Sometimes he wanted back issues of the *Scholastic.*" He made an impatient gesture. "I suppose those contained Zahm materials. Reports of a talk he had given on campus, perhaps the transcript of a lecture. I'll check."

"You keep a record of what materials anyone asks for?"

"Of course."

Roger hummed for a moment, then began to speak as if to himself. It was not impossible, he said, that Kittock did not understand the rules governing use of archival material. Greg might be shocked at the thought, but it could well be that Kittock just took a folder of letters in order to peruse them overnight. "In that case, they will be right back where they belong tomorrow morning."

"Tomorrow is Sunday."

"Well, Monday, then. Of course, if you can't bear to wait you could talk to Kittock."

"*Moi?*" Greg laid a hand on his chest. He seemed relieved to be able to appeal to his speech impediment.

"Do you know where he's staying?" Boris asked.

Greg didn't know. Since he hadn't asked Eggs to register, there would be nothing in the archives to tell them where he was staying. Boris said nothing. The upshot of the meeting was that they would wait out the weekend and see if the letters were back in the appropriate box on Monday morning.

84

Boris had hoped for more than this. In the Morris Inn he called the Jamison Inn and asked for Mr. Kittock.

"One moment, sir."

He listened to the phone ring, wanting to hear Eggs answer so he could hang up on him, but the phone was not answered. He put his briefcase on the desk and opened it. Inside was a folder from the archives. All he had to do now was plant it in Eggs's room and the campus would be too hot for him. Then Boris could proceed with his great plan to realize enough from the sale of Zahm items to get his own finances in order. The diary alone would command a pretty sum.

He opened the desk drawer and put his hand inside, groping about, wanting the reassuring feel of the package that spelled his return to financial health. But nothing met his questing hand. He pulled the drawer entirely free and looked at its rectangular emptiness. The plastic bag and the diary that it had contained were gone.

The mirror above the desk reflected his dumbfounded expression. Then he grabbed the phone and asked the operator to connect him with Professor Knight's apartment. The Morris Inn was part of the university telephone system. After a pause, a ringing began. Phil Knight answered, thank God.

"You're a private investigator."

"Who is this?"

"I'm sorry. Boris Henry. I want to hire you. I've been robbed."

17 "HAVE HIM CHARGED WITH STALK-
ing," Marjorie advised. "If you're sure,
that is."

"Of course I'm sure," Bernice said. "Every time I turn
around, there he is."

"It must be love," Marjorie said, and sighed. "If a husband
can be in love." She was getting a little tired of Bernice going
on about the men in her life. A few days ago it had been the
fascinating man she had run into, a writer, doing work somewhere in the library.

"We talked and talked." Bernice's eyes lifted and seemed
to lose their focus.

"About what?"

"We found we had a lot in common."

"You say he's middle-aged?"

"Middle-aged! I never said that. He's older than we are,
sure. But still youthful."

That had been bad enough to, listen to, but now Bernice
claimed that her former husband, the immigrant, was following her around.

"I suppose he's seen you with your middle-aged lover."

Bernice was too absorbed to be annoyed by this. "He confronted him!" She leaned toward Marjorie, eyes wide. "On a campus sidewalk, people all around. And that's not all."

"Tell me," Marjorie said without enthusiasm.

"He followed me to the Morris Inn, where Eggs and I and a friend of his were having a drink—"

"Eggs?"

"For X. Well, anyway . . ."

Marjorie wore a fixed smile through the narrative. Why were all these interesting things happening to a skinny little thing like Bernice?

"Maybe you could talk your Mr. Eggs into having Ricardo's green card revoked."

"Oh, Marjorie." But Bernice seemed to like it now when Marjorie knocked Ricardo.

"Maybe get him deported as an undesirable alien."

"He's as much of an American as I am."

"Where did you emigrate from?"

"So how are things with you?"

Meaning, how was her love life. The problem was, there wasn't much to tell, unless she stretched a point here and there, as she did when she whispered about the pawing professor at IUSB. It became so vivid as she talked that Marjorie herself almost believed that the harmless old codger who taught real estate law—she was back to her original ambition—had fondled her, cooing in her ear as he patted her bottom.

"Where did this happen?"

"He got me into the phone booth with the excuse that he couldn't read the directory."

"You were in a phone booth with him?"

Marjorie began to think that she should take up writing fiction. It seemed a way of making her life at least a little bit interesting.

Afterward, she thought of telephoning Ricardo, but she was afraid he would hang up on her when she told him who it was. So she parked across from where he was living late Saturday afternoon. She hadn't been there fifteen minutes when his pickup pulled in to the curb. He hopped out and ran up the steps to the front door. Marjorie's heart was in her mouth. Good Lord, he was handsome. For an immigrant.

She guessed he wasn't going to sit around his rented room on a Saturday night, and she was right. He had changed when he came out, nothing dressy, and lit a cigarette when he settled behind the wheel of the pickup. Then he started the engine. Marjorie had the sudden fear that he had a date with someone, but he drove to a sports bar. Marjorie knew that because she followed in her car.

There was an opening at the bar, but Marjorie didn't want to squeeze into it and call attention to the fact that she was alone. All around the place television screens brought in athletic contests, but most were captioned; the noise was in the bar itself, talk, talk, laughter, thank-God-it's-Friday laughter.

Marjorie hoisted herself onto a stool at a high table. There were two women already at the table, but they ignored her. The waitress didn't. She ordered a Bloody Mary.

"Do you want a menu?"

"Not yet."

She could see where Ricardo had settled at the end of the bar. She felt a bit like a stalker herself, keeping an eye on him. He was alone and seemed intent on staying that way. Marjorie let ten minutes go by and then, with her drink in hand, walked along the bar, prepared to be surprised when she ran into him.

"Well, hi," she said.

He sat sidesaddle on the bar stool, and his expression was not encouraging.

"Marjorie," she reminded him.

"I know who you are."

"Are you and Bernice back together again?"

"Why do you ask?"

"I couldn't believe it when you two broke up. You were my model of what a marriage ought to be."

He moved so she could squeeze in next to him at the bar. He offered her a cigarette. "I seem to remember you smoke."

"Where there's fire," she said, and dipped toward the lighter. She hadn't smoked for months, and when she inhaled she nearly passed out.

"Why don't you sit on this stool."

"I'm no mountain climber."

He picked her up and set her on the stool as if she were

light as a feather. She nearly dropped her cigarette, she was so surprised. His face was only inches from hers when he lifted her. She wouldn't mind getting him into a phone booth.

"Do you ever see Bernice?" he asked.

"Oh, no, you don't. I'm not going to sit here and listen to you talk about your ex-wife."

He shook his head. "The divorce doesn't mean a thing. I'm Catholic."

Weren't they all? But Marjorie's bigotry was seeping away. Hadn't Bernice said Ricardo was from Argentina? Marjorie wasn't sure where that was, exactly, but it was definitely way south of the Rio Grande. There was also the cheery thought that here she was, having a drink with Bernice's former husband, whatever he thought, while Bernice was mooning over some middle-aged man.

"I have to tell you I was always jealous of Bernice," Marjorie said.

"I thought we weren't going to talk about her."

"I'm talking about you."

He ordered a hamburger, but Marjorie wasn't hungry. "I'll just nibble on your french fries," she said, giving him a sultry look.

Hours later, after four beers, he got sentimental and wanted to talk about little Henry. "You poor guy," Marjorie said, putting her arm over his shoulders. She was feeling pretty sentimental herself. But then he was back on Bernice.

"There's another guy," he said angrily.

"There always is."

"Not when the woman is my wife!"

They were back to square one. Not that Marjorie would call it wasted time. They left separately; he seemed not to catch her hint that he might follow her to her place. Even so, it was a pleasant evening. Maybe she could tell Bernice that now Ricardo was stalking her.

18 LARRY DOUGLAS HAD BEEN TAKEN on by Notre Dame campus security, thus fulfilling his ambition to get a job on campus. Growing up in South Bend made it impossible not to be aware of the university on the north edge of town. Even if he could have afforded it, Larry was no student. Still, he felt more part of the university than any student could. They were there, what, four years, and then sayonara. Larry's memories of Notre Dame went back to childhood. He had gone over the fence of the golf course and learned the game with one eye out for the ranger. He had sold programs at football games, which was as good as having a ticket. And he had hung around the campus, feeding the ducks down by the lake, walking around the paths, kicking a ball around the soccer fields, a lonely figure on the deserted summer campus. He had put in an application as soon as he graduated from high school, and now, finally, he had been hired.

There are rungs on the ladder of campus security, and Larry was on the lowest. He wore a uniform and a weirdo plastic helmet and pedaled around the campus on a bike giving out parking tickets. Oh well, it was a beginning. The nice thing about tickets was that there was no quota, and who was to say when a lot or a few violations took place? This gave Larry the sense that, low as he was on the totem pole of security, he was his own boss. Wrote his own ticket, you might say. Meanwhile, Laura had been put behind a counter in the old building across from Rockne where security was housed until the new building was ready. Laura was bored skinny.

"I told you," Larry said.

"What did you tell me?"

"Okay, you forgot."

You could say Laura was his girl, though that didn't mean much. When he dreamed of women, Laura didn't enter the picture. There was a lot of her, and she could have used the exercise on the bicycle. Larry thought she had actually gained weight since that day they'd both been hired. The weight and the tattoo put Larry off.

He was no prize, he knew that, but he took care of himself, and he sure as hell didn't have a tattoo on his rear end.

He had been startled when she showed it to him. He danced away. "I'll call a cop."

"I thought you were one." She dug him in the ribs.

The great thing in Laura's favor was that she was affectionate. When they sat for hours in his car at night he felt that she had a wrestler's hold on him, and she groaned a lot, but what the heck, women are different from men. Larry's fear was that Laura would wrestle him up the aisle, and then his life would really settle into a rut.

His great secret was that he liked poetry. What had hooked him at first? Maybe the verse on a birthday card when he was nine, but then he looked into the *Golden Treasury of Poetry* his mother had had since she was a kid. She let Larry have it, and it became his bedside book. Most of the poems were pretty hard to follow, but some were as easy as a greeting card. Like Emily Dickinson. Larry loved Emily Dickinson. He studied the little photograph of her in the back of the book and couldn't figure her out. She seemed to be wearing a First Communion dress, but she was too old for that.

It was Monday morning when Larry emerged from the headquarters of campus security. Laura was already behind the desk, complaining about this and that. Larry didn't put on his helmet until he was outside. He felt like a damned fool wearing the thing, or an alien in *Star Wars*. He threw his leg over the bike and pushed off, heading toward the lake.

Spring just couldn't make up its mind to put in an appearance. It was an overcast day, and there was enough of a wind to make riding a bike twice the work. On the lake, mean-looking waves tumbled the ducks around. Larry went zigzagging along the road to the firehouse, then took a right. The cars in the crescent next to Flanner belonged to people who worked in the North Dining Hall. He could have ticketed them all, but what the heck. He took the sidewalk past the entrance of Flanner and then braked when he came to an area where benches faced one another. A man was sitting there.

Larry touched his helmet in salute, but there was no response from the man. He just sat there, staring straight ahead.

"You feeling all right?" Larry asked. He straddled the bike, his feet on the ground. Still nothing. He leaned down and waved, but the man just kept staring. His radio crackled, and he could hear Laura talking to someone.

"Hey," Larry cried, but still the man didn't budge.

Irked now, Larry put down the kickstand of his bike and went over to the bench. He laid a hand on the man's shoulder, and the fellow just tipped to the side, lying down on the bench. Larry put his hand on the man's forehead. It was ice cold. His first impulse was to get the hell out of there, but then he remembered he was campus security. He plucked his radio from his belt and called in to Laura.

"Laura," he began, and his voice sounded like a kid's. He cleared his throat. "Laura, this is Larry. There's a dead man on a bench in front of Grace."

"Ha ha."

"Damn it. I'm serious. Do something, will you?"

"What?'

"Send someone over here. Right now!"

He signed off and then stood there as if he were on sentry duty, waiting for reinforcements. The guy was middle-aged. A professor? Larry's great fear was that someone would come along before Laura got word to a cruiser. It didn't make any sense, but Larry felt responsible for the dead guy. He just didn't want to look at him.

PART TWO

GOLD LEAF

1   ANY POSSIBILITY OF TENSION AND rivalry between Notre Dame security and the South Bend police department was lessened by the fact that a good many members of the former had put in their time and retired from the latter. Double dippers. Their pension and their Notre Dame salary. But it was Crenshaw, who had served his time on the Elkhart force, who was there at the bench to meet the contingent from downtown. Jimmy Stewart from homicide was in charge. He acknowledged Crenshaw's greeting, but he was already taking in the scene. It was now 8:20 A.M. He looked around.

"What is it, a holiday?"

"How do you mean?"

"Where is everybody?"

"Oh, it's still early here. Things don't begin until maybe nine."

Jimmy shook his head and turned to the bench. The 911 wagon had rolled right across the lawn to the bench where the body was, and the coroner's assistant, Feeney, had just officially pronounced the dead man dead.

"What of?" Stewart asked.

"I'm not sure."

"Take a guess."

"A heart attack?"

Jimmy Stewart groaned. A heart attack! Then what the hell was South Bend homicide doing on the scene? Crenshaw seemed to be avoiding his eyes.

"Who's Flash Gordon?" Jimmy asked him.

"Who?"

Jimmy indicated the young guy straddling the bike and wearing a futuristic helmet.

"He found the body," Crenshaw said. "Hey. Douglas. Come here."

Not only did the kid have to wear that silly helmet, he wore wraparound sunglasses, too, a precaution in case the sun ever put in an appearance. Douglas saluted when he came up to Stewart and Crenshaw. Because of the glasses, it was hard to tell if the kid was smarting off.

"He's new," Crenshaw explained.

"You found the body?" Stewart asked.

"Yes, sir."

"Tell him everything you know," Crenshaw ordered.

It wasn't much of a choice, but Jimmy would take the kid over Crenshaw any day. He took his sleeve and led him away from the activity around the bench. Crenshaw got the hint and didn't follow. Jimmy got out his cigarettes and lit up.

"This is a smoke-free campus," the kid said, but he grinned.

"I forgot to bring my sunglasses," Jimmy said.

The kid took off the wraparounds. He looked even younger.

"When did you start working here?"

"This is my second week."

And this was Monday.

"Was he lying on his side like that?"

"No, he was sitting up straight. When he didn't answer, I only touched his shoulder, and he tipped onto his side."

"He hasn't moved since?"

"No."

A nice kid. Maybe not too smart, but nice. "You like the job?"

"Not this morning."

"Well, there shouldn't be too much of this." Jimmy flipped his cigarette in a high arc into a shrub.

"Three-pointer," the kid said.

Feeney was still checking out the body. If coroners wore helmets like the kid's, you could pick them out of a crowd. Of course, Feeney's shaved head was helmet enough. Once he started to lose his hair he had decided to take baldness by storm, making a preemptive strike with his razor. He stood up, his head white as a mushroom, and looked around. When he saw Jimmy he hurried over.

"It wasn't a heart attack."

Jimmy just waited.

"I mean it wasn't just a heart attack. Come on, I'll show you."

Feeney talked all the way to the body. Everyone was freeze-framed because of what Feeney had found. The dead man was now in a seated position. Feeney put a finger on the shirt collar, pulled it down, and invited Jimmy to inspect the bruise marks on his throat.

"Geez! I never noticed those." It was Douglas, the space cadet.

"I missed it myself at first," Feeney said.

Stewart went through the pockets. There was nothing but lint to be found. No ID. So who was the dead man? He was carted off to the morgue as John Doe. His clothes would be checked out for an indication of who he was, but that would take time. Jimmy could have put the body completely out of his mind, consigning the matter to the routine work of underlings, if it weren't for those bruise marks and the fact that the man had apparently been killed on the campus of Notre Dame. Later, he did make a call to Feeney to make sure that the bruises meant the man had been strangled.

"Not necessarily," Feeney said.

"Yeah?"

"That young man on campus security found a plastic bag in a trash receptacle not far from the body. The kind shirts come back from the dry cleaners in. I'll have tests run on it."

2 ⟶ THE VERSION OF THESE EVENTS
that became official in Notre Dame se-
curity was due to Crenshaw, who had left the scene early and
found the circumstances of the death similar to several in-
stances in the past. Some homeless guy wanders onto the
campus and is found frozen to death the following morning.

"In April?"

"The point is, he doesn't belong here, but anyone can walk
onto the campus. He settles on a bench and bingo, the big
one."

"A heart attack?"

"Isn't that what the coroner thought, Douglas?"

"Before he found the marks on his neck."

"What marks?"

"And there's also the plastic bag I found in a trash receptacle."

"No one mentioned that stuff to me. They're pulling your
leg, kid."

The kid went outside, put his leg over his bike, adjusted his
helmet, and rode away.

———

Phil Knight hadn't golfed since January in Florida, and he wanted to limber up. He arranged to meet Jimmy Stewart at a driving range on 31, nearly to Niles, but he had already hit a couple of buckets of balls before Jimmy showed up. So he took a breather. Watching Jimmy, he might have told him what was wrong with his swing, but friends let friends drive in peace. On the way back, they stopped for a beer.

"You hear about the body on campus, Phil?"

"There are roughly ten thousand bodies on campus."

"The dead one."

"When?"

"This morning."

Jimmy told Phil most of it.

"Why was homicide there?"

Jimmy told him of the marks on the guy's neck and the plastic bag. "The coroner calls it an assisted heart attack."

"Who was he?"

Jimmy shrugged. "We're working on it. All his pockets were empty."

"And there were marks on his neck. Marks like bruises?"

"Feeney."

"Ah."

"Another?"

Phil shook his head. "Got to go." No need to tell Jimmy about the phone call from Boris Henry.

"You want to hire a detective to find a diary?" he had said when Boris Henry explained why he was calling.

"Your brother can explain it to you. The diary is Father Zahm's!"

"Just a minute."

Roger actually rose from his chair when Phil told him why Boris Henry was calling. That was enough for Phil. He went back to the phone.

"Are you at the Morris Inn?"

"Yes. Will you come here?"

"Tonight?"

A pause. "In the morning?"

"At the crack of dawn."

"How about Monday? At eleven o'clock?" Henry's voice had become thoughtful, as if he were embarrassed by his earlier tone of panic.

Phil agreed and hung up.

Roger lumbered in from the study. "I'll come with you."

"Monday morning. He thought about eleven."

Roger was surprised. On Roger's face, expressions always had the look of primary colors. He stared at his brother. "Didn't he sound worried?"

"In a panic. At first. He calmed down."

Roger thought about it. "I suppose there isn't much we could do tomorrow."

We. Phil put his arm around Roger's shoulders. Well, around most of them. The Knight Brothers ride again.

When Phil got home from the driving range, Roger was at his computer. Father Carmody had called, and Phil dialed the priest's number.

"A body was found on campus early this morning, Phil."

"I heard."

"Who told you?"

"Jimmy Stewart."

"In homicide?" The old priest's voice became more un-oiled than usual when he said this.

"They seem to think he was strangled."

There was a long pause. "Who was he?"

"John Doe. There was nothing in his pockets."

"I don't like it. What else did Stewart say?"

Phil repeated the account he had been given.

Father Carmody said, "Campus security thinks he was a hobo who came onto campus in the night and died."

"After emptying his pockets?"

"I don't like it."

For Father Carmody, Notre Dame was a sacred place, and any threat of bad publicity bothered him. He asked Phil to keep in touch with Jimmy Stewart. "You will be liaison for the university on the usual terms."

Phil agreed. Not that there seemed much danger of bad publicity. Whether or not he had been strangled, John Doe would doubtless be consigned to a pauper's grave and soon forgotten.

"Of course, I'll remember the man in my Mass," Carmody said before hanging up.

Roger was the Catholic, not Phil, and Phil still hadn't gotten used to remarks like that. He went into the study. "We've got two cases."

Roger seemed distracted while Phil told him the story. Phil

held back the plastic bag until the end, his punch line, but Roger did not react.

Twenty minutes later, he came out of his study. "I just talked to Greg Walsh. If you'll take him to the morgue, he'll look at the body."

"Does he know who it might be?"

"It's my hunch. Don't blame Greg if it draws a blank."

Few people ever see the morgues in hospitals, let alone the county morgue, though the ultimate refrigerators await us all. Phil's career as a private investigator had involved him in a significant number of violent deaths; he had seen morgues here and there around the country, but different as they were, they all brought the same thought. How many people really believe that one day they will be dead? It was the kind of thought he could express to Roger and to practically no one else. Jimmy Stewart would think he was losing it. Roger just nodded in comprehension.

"Memento mori."

"Gesundheit."

"Monks used to keep a skull in their cell, as a reminder."

"Where did they get it?"

"When conquering heroes paraded through Rome, someone kept whispering in their ear that they were mortal."

"Cheery."

"You brought it up, Phil." For a moment, Phil thought his brother was going to talk to him about becoming a Catholic.

Roger never did, though, and Phil didn't know whether he was relieved or resented it. Sometimes he thought he might raise the subject with Father Carmody.

"Do I pick Walsh up at the library?"

"He said he'd come here."

"Just so he doesn't talk my ear off. You should come along, Roger." Walsh could talk with Roger around.

"I intend to."

Walsh sat in the back of the van with Roger. A swivel chair was rigged up there, large enough for Roger and giving him the advantages of a turret gunner. Of course, there was a computer within reach.

Phil called Boris Henry when they were under way. "It will have to be later than eleven."

"Now see here . . ."

Phil passed the cell phone to Roger, who finally figured out how to use it. "Boris? Roger Knight. A body was found on campus this morning, and my brother and I have to run an errand concerning it. We will be with you as soon as possible."

"Roger, we are talking about the diary of Father John Zahm."

"I understand."

"It is priceless."

"Exactly. That is why nothing is going to happen to it."

"Happen to it! It's been stolen."

"I meant until we get it back."

Phil stayed in Feeney's office while the assistant coroner took Roger and Greg Walsh into the depths. Feeney had given Phil his notes. Phil saw that he was putting the time of death six to eight hours before the discovery of the body. Say midnight. Phil wondered what he had been doing at midnight. Sleeping, that's what. Did he think that his life was connected with the dead man's? Maybe all human lives were connected. Phil shook the thought away. The morgue was exerting its usual effect.

When Roger and Greg returned with Feeney, John Doe was no longer John Doe.

"His name was Xavier Kittock," Roger said, sparing Walsh the effort.

Kittock had been doing research in the archives for a couple of weeks. An alumnus. Father Carmody would be interested in knowing that. It would be surprising if he didn't remember the man from when he was a student.

From the morgue they went to Jimmy Stewart's office.

"He's been on campus for two weeks?" Stewart asked Walsh.

"Working in the archives." It took a while for Walsh to get this out.

"So where was he staying?"

A rhetorical question. Jimmy was indicating that he had a lead of sorts. Phil dropped Walsh off at the library and continued home with Roger, where he got on the phone and called around to local motels. His sixth call was to the Jamison Inn.

"Would you like me to ring his room?"

"Yes."

Phil waited. Had the guy been wearing a wedding ring? He hadn't noticed. He listened to the phone ringing in a room in the Jamison Inn, hoping it wouldn't be answered by a wife or someone. It wasn't. So he called Father Carmody.

"Class of '74," Carmody said, after consulting the hard drive of his memory.

"You remember him?"

"He used to send me postcards when he was in the navy. He put in over twenty years."

That was a bit of information Phil would pass on to Jimmy.

The doorbell rang, and Phil answered it.

"I'm Rebecca. Your brother called and asked me to come over."

Phil remembered her, but it wasn't until Roger came out of his study and took the girl into a bear hug that Phil remembered that she was the niece of Xavier Kittock.

"I'm off to the Morris Inn, Roger."

His brother nodded. "Of course." There was a trace of regret in his voice.

3   IN THE UNIVERSITY CLUB THE OLD
Bastards table was still occupied at 2:30,
much to the chagrin of the staff, who wanted to get out of there
for a few hours before the dinner rush. In the lobby, Pete
Grande and Paul Conway were discussing club business.
Debbie, the hostess, had learned about the identification of
the body, and she brought the news to the table. They had ordered another round of drinks even though no one was sure he
remembered the man.

"Those damned benches are a mixed blessing." The
benches, set along the campus walks at intervals, each bore a
little plaque commemorating the donor. That made them a
mixed blessing for Armitage Shanks.

"Listen, they are one innovation that is unequivocally
good."

"They make me feel like a guest," Shanks complained.

A murmur around the round table. A major grievance with
emeriti was that they soon became strangers on the campus
where they had spent their careers. The lack of institutional
memory was a recurrent theme.

"They should be dedicated to retired professors."

"Some are."

"They all should be!"

"You could sponsor one for yourself."

"And have a fool for a client?"

"Don't be so hard on yourself."

Debbie joined them, taking a chair. "Do you all intend to take your naps here? We want to get the place ready for tonight."

Someone asked what members had their dinner here. The Old Bastards were day persons to a man.

"Lots of townies."

Another groan. Opening club membership to local residents was another grievance. At the outset, the place had been called the Faculty Club.

Debbie asked if any of them had known the dead man. "He was an alumnus."

"All alumni are mortal."

"I may have had him in class," Goucher said, and his milky eyes seemed to search the past.

"How many students do you remember by name?"

"You'd be surprised."

"Indeed I would."

With Shanks it was a point of honor not to remember the names of students. Let them remember him, that was his view. A professor in front of the class was a lot easier to remember than rows of students who changed every semester yet always seemed anonymously the same.

When Debbie stood and then remained beside the table, drinks were drained and chairs began to be pushed back. The old men were always docile with Debbie, and she in turn liked them, more or less. Once she had addressed the Old Bastards as "OB's" and was misunderstood. More than one embarked on a diet.

Goucher asked Debbie to give him his walker. He went first, of course, to ensure that the recessional would be prolonged.

"I suppose he'll be buried here," Debbie said in the lobby.

"Welcome to the club."

4 REBECCA LISTENED TO WHAT Roger Knight told her about Uncle X, and her first thought was that she had to call her father. She felt more empty than sad, confused, and she couldn't cry. It had been kind of fun having X on campus. He had always been more of a rumor than a fact in the family, off in the navy to exotic places. And he never married. A girl in every port? She remembered the young woman she had seen at the Morris Inn with X. She had found it kind of funny that he denied knowing the woman. Imagine a grown man being that bashful. Or maybe he just didn't want Rebecca to think he was human. It was hard to imagine her uncle as a ladies' man, no matter the incident on the campus walk. Rebecca hadn't heard of that, so Roger told her.

"The woman was married?"

"Oh, I'm sure he was just being nice to her. She works in Grace."

"But the man threatened him?"

Suddenly Rebecca saw the significance of this. Her eyes widened as she looked at Roger, but he didn't say what she was sure he was thinking.

"Phil will look into it," he said instead.

"He was staying in the Jamison Inn?"

"Yes."

"What was he writing?" Roger asked.

"Was he writing something?"

"Wasn't he doing research?"

Rebecca thought about it. She never did get a straight answer from him about what he was doing on campus. Research? What did that mean? It would have been more plausible if he had told her he was enrolling in graduate school. "It could have had to do with Notre Dame sports. He was a total fan."

"Isn't everyone?"

"Are you?"

"Indirectly." He meant his brother.

"I have to call my father."

Roger pushed his phone toward her, rising from his special chair. He shuffled out of the room, and Rebecca sat for a moment. She actually had to think to remember her parents' phone number. Her mother answered.

"Mom? Beckie." And then, like an idiot, she began to cry.

"What is it, sweetheart?"

"Uncle X. He's dead."

"Oh my God."

She managed to tell her mother what she knew. Her mother got her father on the line, and then the three of them talked.

"What exactly happened?" her father asked. He tried to sound brisk and businesslike, but there was the sound of her mother crying. Her little brother was dead.

"They found him this morning on a bench on campus."

"On a bench?"

The story seemed to rob Uncle X of any dignity.

Then her father was making plans to fly to South Bend earlier than they had planned. "We'll both come," her mother put in. They would leave the details of their travel plans on her answering machine, they said.

"Are you all right, Beckie?"

"Of course. I'm calling from Professor Knight's. He gave me the news."

Her father said, "Let me talk to him."

Rebecca went in search of Roger Knight and stayed in the living room while he went back to his study. She looked around at the bookshelves. There were bookshelves in every room, and his office in Brownson was four walls of books. Rebecca thought of all the things she didn't know. At the moment, she felt that she didn't know anything. Her uncle was dead, and that seemed to drain everything from her mind.

Roger came out of his study. "You can stay here."

"Oh, I can't do that."

"Do you have classes today?"

"Continental epistemology."

He widened his eyes and lifted his brows. Then she thought of Josh. Why skip class when she had a chance to talk with Josh afterward?

5 "WELL, IF YOU'D COME EARLIER we couldn't have had a drink."

Boris Henry said this as he led Phil into the bar at the Morris Inn. No one else was there. The early afternoon sun slid through the blinds from the courtyard outside, illuminating the pictures on the wall, which featured famous coaches. Phil studied them while Boris brought their drinks from the bar, heading for a table far in back.

Having folded himself into a chair, he lifted his Bloody Mary in a toast. After taking a sip, he leaned toward Phil, looking earnest. "I'm sure Roger told you how valuable the stolen item is."

"Where was it stolen from?"

"Right here. From my room. Like a damned fool, I put it in the desk drawer. When I found it wasn't there Saturday night, I called you right away. I suppose I sounded panicked. Well, I am. Calling such a thing valuable doesn't nearly cover it."

"Who knew you had the diary?"

Henry nodded. "I've thought of that. The provost and Rasp, a man in the foundation. Your brother, of course. And whoever they might have told. But I think I know who did it."

Phil waited.

"A former roommate of mine is on campus." He took another swallow of his Bloody Mary. "How much do you know about Father Zahm?"

"Not much. What should I know?"

"Zahm was fascinated by the search for El Dorado, the legendary city of gold in South America. I won't tell you how many different expeditions set out to find it. Spanish, German, even Sir Walter Raleigh. The only gold involved was that they spent in a fruitless search."

"A legend?"

Henry sat back. "A dream of greed. That is how Zahm sums it up, much as he admired the sense of adventure behind those expeditions."

"He wrote about it?"

"He did. A little book meant to close the book on it. That is why the diary is so interesting."

"How so?"

"Despite what he published, Zahm was convinced El Dorado existed." Another sip from his Bloody Mary. It was like punctuation. "He had found it."

"Come on."

"It's all in the diary, and that makes it valuable in the usual sense, not just historically. My thought is that Notre Dame can finance a final and successful expedition."

"Couldn't you do that yourself?"

"Of course, but it would be like depriving my alma mater of an inheritance Zahm meant for it."

"And you think your former roommate took it."

Boris Henry looked around the room. "Just the other night

we had a drink together here. Right over there." He pointed. "We sat there, the three of us." He shook his head, then finished his drink. "You want another?"

"You go ahead. I'm fine."

Boris Henry stood and went to the bar with giant steps. He leaned toward the bartender as he ordered, and Phil found himself admiring the drama with which Henry told his tale. He still hadn't mentioned his roommate's name.

When he came back, he went farther afield, telling Phil of his proposal that the university establish a John Zahm Center. "Of course, the diary would be meant for the center. That's what I was talking to the provost and the man in the foundation about. They are interested."

"In the search for El Dorado, too?"

"I haven't told them what the diary contains."

"Ah."

"But Xavier Kittock knew."

Phil just looked at Boris Henry. Silence, too, is sometimes golden.

"I'll tell you about him."

So Phil was told the story of Kittock's involvement in a search for sunken treasure. He had come to Kansas City, and Henry, like a fool, had told him about the diary.

"And then I find he has been here, in the archives, doing research in the Zahm papers. Letters that cover the period of the diary are missing."

"From the archives?"

"A whole folder of them from a box Kittock had been studying."

"Do they know this at the archives?"

"I told them. I was the one who discovered that a folder was missing."

"Told who?"

"A man named Greg Walsh."

"I know him. He's a friend of Roger's."

"And now he's stolen the diary of John Zahm."

"Have you confronted him on this?"

"Why don't you and I call on him?" A man with a mission, Henry rose and headed for the door.

"Where do you suppose he is?" Phil followed.

"Not in the archives. I called, and the director said he wasn't there. He is staying at the Jamison Inn."

"Have you called there?"

"I want to surprise him."

"When you said you had a drink with him the other night, you said 'the three of us'"

"He had gotten hooked up with a waitress while he was here. After a while she left, and we sat on."

It was when they were crossing the lobby that Boris was distracted by excited chatter. A dead body had been found on campus and now had been identified. Boris got to a chair and slumped into it. Phil stood before him. Boris looked up at Phil, and then his expression changed.

"You knew that already, didn't you?"

"Yes."

"And didn't tell me."

"You didn't give me an opportunity."

Henry thought about that, as if reviewing their conversation in the bar. Reluctantly, he conceded that Phil was right.

"When would you have told me?"

Phil shrugged.

"When we got to his hotel room?"

"Oh, I would have advised against that. The police will be examining his room."

6   BERNICE HEARD THE NEWS WHEN she came to work that morning, but the body had not yet been identified, so it was just a spooky story everyone wanted to talk about. From the windows of the restaurant she could see the bench where the body of the man had been found. Hadn't she sat there with Xavier? She hadn't—they had usually sat at an outside table—but still it gave her a nice tingly feeling. She couldn't wait to tell him when he came for lunch.

There seemed to be a rush on Grace that day. The place was swarming with people, and everyone seemed to be talking about the dead man. It was a little ghoulish, although Bernice was looking forward to doing just that with Xavier. But he didn't come. Maybe the story kept him away. Martha at the cash register kept looking at Bernice, and finally Bernice went over there to see what it was all about.

"They know who it was," Martha said.

"Who?"

"The man who ate here and always stayed late. You know."

Bernice just stared at Martha.

"His name was Kittock."

Bernice went back into the dining area and began to clear tables. She tried to make her mind a blank. Every time she had seen him, every time they had talked, came back so vividly that she could not drive the memories away. Martha was following her with a concerned look, and this conferred an importance on Bernice she kind of liked. Of course, Martha and others would have noticed that she had become friendly with Kittock. It made her almost a widow.

What she remembered most was the time they had sat together at a table outside the Morris Inn, in the back, with the big white reception tent billowing in the wind. It was the closest thing they had ever had to a date. Then that girl had come along, and he had abandoned Bernice. Thank God his friend had invited her to have a drink with them.

"My niece," he explained the following day.

"I felt like an idiot after you left. You might have introduced us."

"Maybe next time."

There would never be a next time, not now.

"I did enjoy our drink together," she said.

Until Ricardo showed up, that is. She dismissed the memory. What Bernice couldn't understand was how she really felt. It didn't seem to be sadness, yet that was what Martha's expression suggested she should feel. So she adopted a solemn expression and went on working. When the lunch period was over she just wanted to go home.

"Are you all right, Bernice?"

"I will be, Martha." She bit her lip. What an actress.

She left Henry in day care. She wanted the rest of the afternoon free. Alone, she could explore her feelings and try them out to see which would be the appropriate one. She began to think she could write a story about Xavier. Then Marjorie called.

"Oh, Bernice!"

"Marjorie?"

"Yes." Marjorie sounded miffed that Bernice hadn't recognized her voice. Of course, she had. "Have you seen him?"

Him? Did Marjorie mean Xavier Kittock? What a weird question. "Of course not."

"Bernice, I ran into him last night. At a sports bar."

"You should tell the police."

"Have the police talked with you yet?"

"Yet? Why should they talk with me?" But now she imagined herself an object of attention, the younger woman Xavier had been so interested in.

"I wonder if you understand how angry he is with you."

"Marjorie, what in God's name are you talking about?"

"Ricardo! Surely you must see—"

Bernice hung up, really angry. What a silly, nosy creature Marjorie was. And what did Ricardo have to do with what had happened to Kittock?

The question followed her through the house. The phone began to ring again, and Bernice ran back, picked it up, and then dropped it into the cradle again. Then she took it off the hook.

Marjorie was suggesting that Ricardo had been so jealous of Kittock that . . . Good Lord. That was impossible. Being macho was one thing, but killing someone was something

124

else. Of course, Ricardo had stopped Kittock on a campus sidewalk and thumped his chest, but what did that mean? And he had surprised her in the Morris Inn when she came out of the bar after having a drink with Eggs and his friend, hustling her through the lobby as if he were arresting her. She waited until they were outside before she kicked him sharply in the shin and ran off to her car.

"You better be careful," he had called after her.

Bernice found that she liked more than she would have admitted the thought that her former husband had decided to avenge himself on Kittock. What would she say if they interviewed her? She meant the television news, not the police. She turned on the set.

Soap operas, but on the hour, local news. The man found dead on the Notre Dame campus had been strangled or perhaps suffocated. A plastic bag had been found. Bernice laughed. She couldn't help herself. It was worse than a soap opera. A comic book. She felt a rush of relief as well. No one would imagine that Ricardo would take his revenge in such a way.

When she went to pick up Henry at day care, Bernice half expected television trucks to be parked along the curb and reporters eager to talk to her, but no one there seemed to have heard of the death on the Notre Dame campus.

"I thought Daddy was coming," Henry said.

"That's tomorrow."

Henry looked disappointed, and that irked Bernice. She worked her fingers to the bone for her boy, and all he did was miss his father.

On the way home, listening to Henry's chatter, she wished she had asked Marjorie just how she had managed to run into Ricardo at a sports bar. It seemed an insult. That was how she and Ricardo had met, as Marjorie well knew.

7 ⟶ WHEN PHIL TOLD JIMMY STEWART
that Kittock had been staying in the
Jamison Inn, they agreed to meet there.

"I drove here along Angela," Jimmy said when he arrived.
"That golf course sure looks inviting."

"I could get us a tee time for tomorrow morning."

"Good. I hope I can make it."

They went to the desk and asked the clerk to call Kittock's
room.

"Have you been trying to reach him?" Jimmy asked.

"Several people have."

"Several."

The clerk nodded, as if his honesty had been impugned.
Well, Phil thought, *one of the several was me.* There was no answer in Kittock's room, of course, so Jimmy showed his ID and
asked to be shown the room.

"Is something wrong?"

"Come on along and see."

The second-floor hallway was almost blocked with cleaning
carts. There was a DO NOT DISTURB sign on the door of 212. The
clerk knocked before unlocking the door and stood aside so

Jimmy and Phil could enter. Jimmy flipped the switch as he went in.

The blinds were drawn, but the bed had not been slept in. On the little desk were some papers and several books, but otherwise the room was neat as a pin, and probably had been since the last time the maid cleaned it. Jimmy went into the bathroom. A pair of pajamas hung on a hook behind the door and toilet articles were neatly arrayed.

Phil was holding one of the books when Jimmy emerged. "I hope only your set of prints will be on that book." Phil dropped it onto the desk, and Jimmy laughed. "What was he reading?"

"A life of Father John Zahm by Ralph Weber."

"Zahm."

"Let Roger explain it to you. That was the man Kittock was reading about in the archives."

The two men stood in silence for a moment, looking around the room. A man now dead had stayed here and had left very little impress on it. Phil moved toward the bed. From a knob on the bedpost a rosary hung. Phil bent over to look. Roger would want to know about that.

The folder of letters from the Notre Dame archives was lying on the desk. Phil said, "I'll take these. Roger can return them to the archives."

Jimmy thought about it, then nodded. "Well, he seems to have been staying here alone."

"Why would you think otherwise?"

"We got a call."

Jimmy told Phil about it downstairs in the bar, where they had Cokes as far from the bartender as they could get. The caller had been a woman evidently trying to disguise her voice. She had said, "If you wonder what happened to Xavier Kittock, you might check with Bernice Esperanza."

"Who is she?" Phil asked.

"That's what we're going to find out after we finish our Cokes."

First, they told the desk clerk that they were finished upstairs.

"Is something wrong?" he asked them.

"You've lost a guest. But don't rent that room until I give the go-ahead."

"Well, thank heavens he had to show a credit card when he registered."

"Let me see that, will you?"

Jimmy had to show his ID again before the clerk slid the registration form across the desk. The impression of the credit card was blurred. A MasterCard. Jimmy jotted down the number. As they pulled out of the parking lot, leaving Phil's car behind, he was reading it to someone downtown who would check it out. That would give them an address.

"I wonder where the card is now? And whatever else was in his wallet," Phil said.

8 — JOSH'S GRANDMOTHER HAD DIED during his freshman year, and he had gone home for the funeral. It had been his first experience with death. What had struck him most was the way people at the wake just stood around and talked, not solemn at all, no one really broken up, not even his father, whose mother she had been. Of course, Grandma had been old, but even so. Josh had gone off from the others and sat at the end of a row of chairs and looked ahead to where his grandmother's profile was just visible over the open coffin. Things quieted down when the priest came and the rosary was said, but as soon as it was over everybody was talking again, even laughing. Josh went up to the casket and knelt and prayed for his grandmother. He wanted to ask her to pardon her family and friends, who seemed to think her death was just another social event.

At least Rebecca seemed stunned when she told him about her uncle. She said it in a whisper, and he wasn't sure he understood, but then she repeated it. "It was his body they found on a campus bench this morning. Had you heard about that?" His expression told her he hadn't.

"Remember, we ran into him the other day."

Of course he remembered. The man had called to Rebecca, and they had talked for a minute or so and then had gone on. She had called him the black sheep of the family.

"My parents are on their way."

At his grandmother's funeral everyone seemed to know what to say to his father and mother, the phrases well worn from other similar occasions. Josh didn't know what to say to Rebecca. He put his hand on her arm.

"I still can't believe it," she said.

"What was it? A heart attack?"

She lifted her shoulders. "I suppose."

They went to the student center and sat in a booth, neither of them wanting anything. Over Rebecca's shoulder a television was visible, blaring on unheeded.

"I told you he never married."

He nodded.

"And that he was in the navy." A wry smile formed on her lips. "Roger Knight told me *he* was in the navy."

Josh had to smile, too. "On our side?"

She put his hand on his. Pretty soon he would be as jolly as the people at his grandmother's funeral.

"I didn't hear a word Tenet said in class," she said.

"I did. It didn't help."

She squeezed his hand. "I hardly know you and I'm dumping all this on you."

"How old was he?"

"He graduated in 1974. I suppose you can figure it from that."

Subtract twenty-one or -two from the current year and it

was clear her uncle had been no kid. He hadn't looked as old as he must have been when they ran into him on campus. It was a strange thought, an alumnus visiting the campus and being found dead on a bench.

The news had come on, and someone turned up the set at the mention of Notre Dame. The story was about the body found that morning on campus. Shots of the area, the bench on which the man had been sitting, and then a photograph.

Rebecca gave a little cry. "That picture's a hundred years old."

The reporter was saying that the police were being very careful in their announcements. "Of course, folks, this is Notre Dame." A faint cheer went up. So much for sarcasm.

Rebecca looked at her watch. "Their plane is due at seven twelve."

Her parents. Should he offer to go with her to pick them up? He would if she asked, but she didn't, and that was a relief.

"That picture they showed? Uncle X was in the navy then, so think how old it is. Would you have recognized the man you met from that picture?"

"Probably not."

"Probably?"

This was a running day, and he had not yet been out, but he didn't want to leave Rebecca alone. He suggested a brisk walk around the lakes.

She jumped at the idea. "I'm not even going to change shoes."

9   SEAN FEENEY LOVED PATHOLOGY, but he hated dead bodies. He had been persuaded during his residency at Mayo that he needn't see a corpse from one year to the next. He would be examining the results of biopsies. He liked the picture of himself as more scientist than physician. It hadn't worked out that way.

He returned to South Bend from Rochester, not because he intended to practice there—he had three offers from clinics in preferable parts of the country—but to relax a bit and show off for his parents. They were proud of him, and he was proud of them for being proud. Who ever thought a Feeney would make it through medical school, let alone have a residency at Mayo? His big mistake was going to his father's political club, which was in a panic mode. Their candidate for coroner had died, and they had twenty-four hours to name a replacement.

"We can put up anyone with name recognition. He doesn't have to be a doctor."

"But who will do the work?"

Casey, the wheeler-dealer, looked at Sean. "Who's this?"

"My son Sean. Dr. Sean."

"Yeah. You teach or what?"

"He is a pathologist."

In retrospect, his father must have seemed to be nominating him for coroner. Did Casey leap with joy at the prospect? He took Mr. Feeney into a corner and frowned while he talked. Sean's father kept shaking his head, and Casey kept grabbing his arm to keep him from getting away. Twenty minutes later Sean was presented with the results of the conference.

"I'm not running for coroner!"

"Assistant coroner," his father said.

"Jankowski will carry you in, doc. Don't worry."

"Tell him what I get," Mr. Feeney said.

Casey smiled benevolently. He had his hand on Sean's sleeve. "Your father here has been a loyal member of the party."

Sean knew all about that. His father would vote for Genghis Khan if he were a Democrat. As a reward for his loyalty, Mr. Feeney would spend his twilight years in a do-nothing position at the waterworks. Just watch the dials and try to stay awake. Casey punched Sean in the arm. The plea in his father's eye was one Sean could not resist.

His mother became hysterical when she heard that Sean was on the ticket. Her son the doctor, playing second fiddle to that idiot Jankowski?

"Tell her the rest, Dad."

Sean went out on the porch. The neighborhood was not what it had been. Maybe his parents should move. Naw. They loved it here on the west side, half a block from church in one direction, half a block from a saloon in the other. All their old friends were here, at least the ones who hadn't moved to the suburbs. He was twenty-nine. Maybe his father's party would lose the election.

That had been two years ago. Jankowski and the rest of the ticket won in a landslide. The victor took over the coroner's office and let Sean do all the work. There had been plenty of work. Where did all these bodies come from? Of course, everybody has to die, but did everyone need an autopsy? The ones that came to Feeney did. Still, he hadn't had a real challenge until the body of Xavier Kittock was found on a bench on campus at Notre Dame.

On the scene, he had thought heart attack. Not stroke. Rigor mortis could mislead you, but Feeney ruled out a stroke. So a heart attack. He didn't chip it in stone, of course. Jimmy Stewart had wanted his guess, and that was what he got. Then Feeney noticed the bruises on the neck.

"Then we got a murder," Stewart said.

"I'm not so sure."

"What do those marks on his throat suggest?"

"Strangling."

"That would be an odd method of suicide."

"You may be right."

"May be. Look, Doc, this is your call. Make up your mind."

In an ideal world, Feeney would have been able to explore all the possibilities. The logical possibilities. His first hunch had been a heart attack, and that seemed to fit a body found on a bench.

"His pockets were empty," Stewart said.

"A thief?"

Stewart shook his head.

"Look, this is more complicated than it seems."

Feeney got out the lab report, but Stewart held up his hand.

"I trust you. So we have a man who had a heart attack while being strangled."

Feeney beamed. "That's a real possibility. I've been thinking the same thing."

"Great minds."

Stewart had a tough time keeping a straight face when he said it, but Feeney accepted it and left. In his office Feeney plunged his hands into the pockets of his lab coat and sat in the chair Jankowski had rejected and Feeney had claimed. It had wheels and turned 360 degrees with one good push of the foot. It was like sitting in a gyroscope, but Feeney found it conducive to thinking.

He had spent long years at Mayo in the expectation that a time would come when people in the operating theater would await his examination of the results of a biopsy. Benign. Malignant. Depending on what he said, the operation would proceed or not. Or take a different tack. Being assistant coroner bore a remote resemblance to that. Jimmy Stewart's investigation depended on his judgment as to the cause of death. There was no doubt that there were bruises on the throat. Even so. So he kept at it. With surprising results.

Douglas, the young man from Notre Dame campus security, called to tell Feeney about the plastic bag he had found in a trash receptacle not ten yards from the body. "You know the kind shirts come it?"

Feeney imagined the scene. A man is sitting on a bench; his assailant approaches from behind, positions himself behind the bench, lifts the plastic bag, and brings it over the sitting man's head.

Douglas said, "There are signs of a struggle."

Feeney reined himself in. "Isn't that bench on concrete?"

"Just off the walkway."

"Signs of struggle?"

Listening to Douglas describe them, Feeney had a sense of the way he himself sounded to Stewart. "About that plastic bag."

"I'll bring it down."

Meanwhile, back to the original guess. The trouble with that was that the heart showed no signs of an infarction. Imagine a court scene. Feeney often did, seeking to restore some sense of drama to his life. He would be called to the stand; life or death hung in the balance. If it came to that with Xavier Kittock, death by heart attack would be ridiculed by the defense. So what was left? Sighing, Feeney asked Kimberley to roll Kittock into the autopsy theater.

Kimberley was only a high school graduate, and her internship was supposed to be a political plum. She almost always wore a mask, and her wide, frightened eyes followed everything Dr. Feeney did with the corpse on the table. When she talked with the mask on, the material made reading her lips easy. She wore a long white garment over her street clothes that looked like an alb, the mask, and then, to top it off, a baseball cap.

Feeney turned on the recording equipment and reexamined the body of Xavier Kittock. Kimberley gagged and left the room when he uncapped the skull. He removed several sections from the brain, restored the skullcap, and called Kimberley back. Her eyes asked if she should take the body back to the cooler.

"Just leave it here."

"You're not done?"

"No."

"What are you looking for?"

"You'll be the first to know."

She had a crush on him, but that was ridiculous. He was eight years older than she was.

In his office, he was thinking of what he should tell Stewart, how he could put it, when the detective strolled in.

"He wasn't strangled," Feeney announced.

Stewart just stood there looking at him.

"The marks on his throat must have been made holding the bag tight so he couldn't breathe."

"Asphyxiation?"

"I doubt it."

"Honest?"

"Cross my heart."

"So it was his heart?"

How do you say yes while retaining the right to say no later? Feeney didn't know. "I guess."

"Guess?"

"There is no damage to the heart."

"He is dead, isn't he?"

Feeney made a face.

"So how the hell did he get that way?"

"I'm working on it."

After Stewart left, Feeney resolved to resign his position and go off to the kind of medical practice he had prepared himself for. Surely they wouldn't take the waterworks job away from his father, the old party loyalist. Then he thought of Casey's dead eyes and knew the man would sell his mother into slavery if political revenge required it.

That was when Kimberley came in, all smiles.

"A fellow from Notre Dame brought this." She handed him a plastic bag.

"Has he gone?"

"I could go after him."

Something in the way she said it gave Feeney a pang.

10 ROGER WAS AS DELIGHTED AS the circumstances permitted when Phil brought him the news of the coroner's vacillation. Of course, Xavier Kittock was still dead—Rebecca's uncle was dead, and her parents had arrived, determined that the funeral should be at Notre Dame.

"Ya es muerto, decid todos, / Ya cubre poca terra." Roger murmured these lines when he was introduced to Rebecca's father, David Nobile. Nobile immediately recognized the lines from *La Dorotea.*

"Of course, you changed the gender." He looked as if he'd like to take Roger off somewhere and talk about the poetry of Lope de Vega. He shook his head. "Terrible about my brother-in-law."

"I never met him."

"It's damned annoying, the way they keep changing the cause of death."

They were in the hallway outside the chapel of Zahm Hall, where Father Carmody would say a Mass for the repose of the soul of Xavier Kittock. The Nobiles were planning to bury him at Arlington, but the body had still not been released by the coroner. Nonetheless, as Father Carmody put it with uncharacteristic rhetorical flourish, Kittock's soul had long since been released from his body, and they could pray for its eternal rest while they awaited the verdict of the coroner.

"When Rebecca called us I thought right away of South America," Nobile said.

Roger stepped back in surprise.

"X had become obsessed with Father Zahm's travels down there," Nobile went on. "One of his books was called *The Quest of El Dorado.*"

"Ah." Roger had read the entire Zahm canon in preparation for his course, but he had to admit that the travel books interested him less than the others, except the one on the Holy Land. Still, he knew Nobile was right. Zahm had been a great admirer of the conquistadores and a gung-ho American as well. No wonder the priest and Teddy Roosevelt had gotten along so well.

Coming toward them with head bowed, wearing a black suit and a mournful expression, was Boris Henry. He nodded to Roger and put out his hand to Rebecca's father. "Henry. Boris Henry. Your brother-in-law and I were classmates."

"Had you kept in touch?"

"Paul Lohman is on his way. He and I and Eggs—Xavier— shared a room in Zahm."

"Eggs?" David Nobile chortled. "That's good. It's even better with his middle name."

"What's that?"

"Benedict."

Roger drifted away, to the degree that such graceful motion can be attributed to a three-hundred-pound man, and found Rebecca and her mother listening to a voluble young woman. Rebecca waved Roger over as if in relief.

"This is Bernice Esperanza. Professor Knight."

"Knight?" Bernice stared at Roger, then grasped one hand with the other, as if she were taking herself into custody. To Mrs. Nobile she said, "You see how rattled they've made me. I think one of the detectives was named Knight."

"Philip Knight?"

She wheeled on Roger. "You know him?"

"Oh, he's notorious."

"He wasn't as bad as the other one, Stewart. They seemed to think . . . I don't know what they thought."

"Why were they pestering you?" Roger asked, though he had already had an account of the visit from Phil. She had inhaled deeply, in preparation for answering, when a bell rang and down the hall Father Carmody appeared, vested to say Mass. In a stage whisper he said they could regard this as a dress rehearsal of the funeral Mass, which he would be saying in Sacred Heart Basilica at a time yet to be arranged.

Roger felt a hand on his arm. Bernice looked at him anxiously. "Can I attend?"

"Of course."

"I'm not Catholic."

"Neither is Philip Knight." He stepped aside for her to go in before him, which she did with a very puzzled expression.

Phil's report on the visit he and Jimmy Stewart had paid to Bernice Esperanza, prompted by an anonymous call to police headquarters, had yielded what at the time seemed important information. Bernice had a former husband who had not taken kindly to her friendship with X. Kittock. In fact, he had as much as threatened him publicly on a campus walk. Roger had heard the same story from Rebecca.

"Why can't he put it all behind him?" Bernice asked the detectives when they brought up her husband.

"I suppose that's like asking why you don't go back to him."

"That's a strange thing to say."

"Would you call your friendship with Kittock a love affair?"

It had been Jimmy's purpose to stir her up, and he certainly succeeded. When he referred to Henry as a latchkey child, she demanded that they leave.

"These are simply routine questions, Mrs. Esperanza."

"But why are you putting them to me?"

"Someone telephoned."

"What?"

"Normally, we don't pass on that kind of information, but in your case it seems appropriate."

She would have liked to ponder the meaning of that, but she was not to be diverted. "And I know who called you."

"Are you sure?"

"Absolutely."

"The call was anonymous."

"It was Marjorie. It couldn't have been anyone else. My friend! Now she's chasing after Ricardo and trying to get me into trouble with the police."

"Marjorie who?"

"Marjorie Waters. Wait, I'll write down her address. Why don't you go over there and bother her for a while."

There was no doubt a sadistic streak in Jimmy Stewart, but then he had been in police work a long time. His wife had left him, just walked out, leaving him an enigmatic note, so Jimmy had developed a pretty low estimate of the female sex.

After the Mass, Roger went out to his golf cart to find Greg Walsh sitting in the passenger seat. He had not yet heard the latest news from the coroner, and Roger filled him in.

"So we might have a natural death, not a murder," Roger concluded.

"That's good."

"It is indeed. Phil and Jimmy Stewart went right to work, as of course they should have, looking for an explanation of Kittock's death. That is, looking for the person who had brought it about. Now, thank God, that can be set aside."

"Well, at least the letters are back," Greg said.

Roger had turned over to Greg the folder Phil had found in Kittock's room. "I'm sure he didn't mean to keep them."

Greg's silence had nothing to do with his speech impediment. Well, one couldn't expect an archivist to be philosophical about scholars walking off with precious materials. After some little while, he said, "I would never have suspected him of such a thing."

Roger told himself that the important thing was that the letters were back where they belonged. Still, their temporary absence nibbled at the edges of his mind.

11

IN THE FOLDER CONTAINING THE returned letters there was a brief biography of the legendary John Zahm.

John Augustine Zahm (1851–1921) came from a farming family that moved from Ohio to Huntington, Indiana, from which town he came to Notre Dame in 1867 at the age of fifteen. Four years later, he received his A.B. degree and soon thereafter entered the Congregation of Holy Cross. Before his ordination in 1875, he held a number of administrative and teaching posts and was something of a protégé of the founder, Father Edward Sorin. His interest in science was evident from the very beginning, but he was as well an extremely cultivated man. Much of the scientific equipment and specimens that he collected went up in smoke when the Main Building burned in 1879, but Zahm, like Sorin, turned immediately to the task of rebuilding. His travels had begun in 1878. With Father Sorin, he toured the Holy Land in 1887. His campus activities, as professor of science and vice president, suggest a whirlwind. Beyond campus, he became known for his insistence that there can be no conflict between science and religion. His attempts to see evolution from a Christian point of view got him into trouble, and he had to rein himself in. Not all of his fellow religious shared his enthusiasms, and when

*Zahm was named provincial of Holy Cross, the effective director
of all the congregation's activities in the United States, he was
subject to constant criticism. In 1906, worn down by the work, he
stepped down and left Notre Dame. For the rest of his life he was
quartered at Holy Cross College in Washington or was traveling.
He had published before, but now came a steady stream of books,
many of them under pseudonyms, such as the anagram H. J.
Mozans. His travels in the southwestern United States had begun
early. Now he turned to the south and undertook some demanding journeys, one in company with Teddy Roosevelt, who became
a friend. Zahm was fascinated by the story of the search for El
Dorado. In recounting that history, he mixed moralizing about
cupidity with a clear admiration for the conquistadores. Zahm
turned what might be construed as years of exile away from
Notre Dame into the opportunity for travel of a kind his colleagues could scarcely have dreamt of. He died in Germany in
1921. His body was brought home to Notre Dame to the community cemetery, where he lies with Father Sorin and others of the
great silent majority of the Congregation of Holy Cross.*

The account was not a photocopy, which told against the sup-
position that Kittock had taken it from a book of reference.

"It is a thin digest of Weber," Boris Henry said.

The fact that the biography was found in the same folder as
the missing but now returned letters seemed adequate explanation of their disappearance. Kittock must have taken the
letters to his room at the Jamison to continue his research on
Father Zahm.

"Odd that he should have emphasized the travels," Roger
said. "No mention at all of Zahm's Dante collection."

"Or of his brother Albert."

"Does El Dorado loom that large in his books?"

"What have I been telling you?" Henry said. "I would call it an obsession. The accounts of his retracing the routes of the various efforts to find El Dorado are harrowing. Why would he have put himself through all that? Certainly not just to lament the folly of other men. He shared that folly. He himself was looking for El Dorado."

"And didn't find it?"

"That remains to be seen."

It was Phil who told Roger that it was clear from Kittock's effects that he and Boris Henry had been in communication about Zahm. In the room were were dozens of printed e-mails, some going back years, and, as if to mark a cultural divide, even older letters.

"I had the impression that they had become strangers to one another."

But when Paul Lohman arrived he assured Roger that the three old roommates had never lost touch, however geographically separate.

"Eggs had to go where the navy sent him, obviously, but e-mail is a marvelous thing. Particularly in recent years, and since Eggs's retirement from the navy, there have been several messages among us every week."

"I got a different impression from Henry."

"He did think Eggs was poaching on his territory."

"In what way?"

"The El Dorado thing. It's funny," Paul Lohman mused. "Neither Eggs nor Boris ever wrote a thing, not even letters once they started using e-mail. Yet both of them were planning books."

"And both on Zahm?"

"They should have collaborated."

Meanwhile, Phil went off with Jimmy Stewart.

"What's up?" Phil asked.

"I thought you'd want to be with me when I speak to Esperanza."

12 WHEN CLARE HEALY ARRIVED, Boris was waiting for her at the Morris Inn. He had booked a room for her after receiving her phone call a few hours earlier. A room on the third floor. Boris was on the second. Discretion is the better part of valor. Boris was a different man on the campus of his old university, but Clare thought this would have been true even apart from the purpose of his visit. The theft of the diary had rattled him less than she would have imagined. He nodded when Clare told him that she had found the news sufficiently disturbing to bring her to South Bend. After all, the diary was an investment by Henry Rare Books.

"I'm glad you're here." He looked away, almost embarrassed by the admission.

She had caught a flight from Kansas City to Chicago Midway and come the rest of the way in a rented car. It was two in the morning when she arrived. Boris waited while she got her key.

"I left my bag in the car."

"I'll get it."

Boris slung his briefcase over his shoulder, and they went together to the parking lot of the inn. Boris opened the passenger door and slid in.

"What's this?" Clare asked him.

"I'll give you directions."

When he told her to pull in at the Jamison Inn, she was confused. "Boris, I just checked in at the Morris Inn."

"I know. Come on."

Inside, he went to the desk and said, "Xavier Kittock."

The heavy-lidded eyes of the clerk lifted from the portable television with which he whiled away the night shift. He turned and took a key from a box and slid it across the desk. A minute later, they were ascending in the elevator. Clare said nothing further. Good Lord, was she remembering New Orleans?

She said, "The clerk thought you were Xavier Kittock."

"That's his problem."

"So what are we going to do, burst in on him?"

"If he's not out out with someone."

He wasn't surprised to find the room empty. All the better.

Inside the room, he turned to her. "You check the bathroom."

"What am I looking for?"

"Clare, you know the diary is missing."

So she checked the bathroom, calling out that she felt ghoulish looking around. He knew how she felt. Then he asked her to come out.

"Did you find anything?" she asked.

He pointed at a folder on the dresser top. "Those are Zahm letters taken from the archives."

"So?"

"You can't take materials from the archives."

"Shame on him."

Once more he slung his briefcase over his shoulder. "Maybe this wasn't a good idea."

"If the diary is here, let's find it."

"This place gives me the creeps."

She put her arm through his. "You're right, let's go."

When they left the room, he pocketed the key, then led her away from the elevators and down the stairs. Soon they were in the parking lot without having passed the desk.

"You must be dead tired, Clare."

"You might have thought of that before."

He put his hand on her arm. "I'm sorry."

She was silent on the drive back to the Morris Inn, as if she were trying to figure out what the meaning of his touching her arm had been.

13 ⟶ LARRY DOUGLAS WAS DOING FIG-
ure eights in the parking lot east of the
library, all but empty at the start of a new day. Crenshaw was
still mad at him for saying that a heart attack had been ruled
out. He had gone back to the crime scene, if it was one, and
managed to get the coroner to admit that he didn't know what
the man had died of but that, sure, it could have been a heart
attack.

"By the time he makes up his mind we'll all be dead." This
was Crenshaw's attempt at a peace offering. Larry didn't bring
up the plastic bag that he had taken down to Feeney.

"It was the way you said it," Laura explained to him.

"How's that?"

"Like you caught Crenshaw in a lie."

Larry gave up, but he had hoped Laura would back him up,
give him some support. Finally she had, last night, grappling
in his car. She had decided she didn't like Crenshaw, who had
said something about her weight.

"If that's a problem, why did they hire me?"

"Bike duty would do it."

"Bah."

Kimberley, the girl in Feeney's office, was not thin either, although compared with Laura . . . When she had come running after him to bring him back to talk with the coroner, he was in uniform but minus that stupid helmet. She seemed impressed by all the things hanging on his belt, especially his weapon. She put her hand gently on the holster, then pulled it immediately away, giving a little shiver.

"How does it feel to walk around with a gun on your hip?"

Since Larry Douglas had been doing this for only two weeks, he himself was very conscious of the fact that he was armed, but, asked, he just shrugged and grinned.

Crenshaw agreed that Larry should visit Feeney.

"It says Jankowski on the door," Larry said.

"I'm assistant coroner," Feeney explained.

"And he does all the work," Kimberley said.

Feeney seemed pleased at her remark. Surely she wasn't interested in a guy that old.

The assistant coroner was explaining the tests he would run on the plastic bag. "Of course, your prints will be on it."

"They're registered."

"Of course."

Feeney sat back and brought the tips of his fingers together, his eyes drifting to the ceiling. This was, he said, an interesting case. He went on, emphasizing the skills that he brought to the task, and Larry wondered why the hell he had come. The recital got easier to sit through when Kimberley exchanged a look with him. Larry settled in his chair and nodded, wanting Feeney to go on. It gave him a chance to look at Kimberley—and to think that as an officer of the law, more or less, he had skills of his own. He tuned out the assistant coro-

154

ner and entertained fantasies of pursuing this interesting case. After all, he had found the body, and it was first of all a campus matter. Crenshaw was an idiot, of course—Larry's Jankowski—and there had been no investigative effort on the part of campus security. The whole thing had been dumped into the laps of the South Bend police, and that had been an end to it.

"Of course, we'll cooperate," Crenshaw had said importantly, "but the powers that be want this thing over and done with."

When Feeney offered to show Larry around his domain, the theater in which he exercised his skills, Larry rose. "I wish I had the time."

Feeney laughed. "Kimberley hates the place."

"It gives me the creeps," she said, as she walked out to the lot with him. His car reminded him of Laura, and Kimberley seemed even more attractive.

"What's it like, working there?" he asked.

"It's a job. Temporary."

"Oh?"

"I'd like to continue my education."

They stood there by his car. Larry rested his hand possessively on a fender but avoided looking at the front seat that had known such passionate interludes with Laura. Then, incredibly, he was telling Kimberley of his love for poetry.

"Do you know Robert Lowell?" she asked.

He could see the photograph of the poet in the back of his *Golden Treasury.* "I would have thought you'd like Emily Dickinson."

"Oh, I love her."

Larry would have liked to recite some poem by the Maid of Amherst, but at the moment he was unable to remember a line. In Kimberley he saw a soul mate. What did he really have in common with Laura other than those silent hours in his car? And campus security, of course.

"We ought to get together," he suggested.

"Okay."

"Tonight?"

"Tomorrow night would be better."

So it was arranged. He drove off to campus with the sense that destiny had just put in an appearance. As he drove, whole poems by Emily Dickinson were ready on his tongue, and he declaimed aloud, "I'm nobody. Who are you? Are you nobody, too?"

The next morning, in the parking lot, making lazy figure eights with his bike, he wondered how he could discover how the man found dead on the bench had got there.

14 ⟶ THIN, GANGLY, HIS MOUSY HAIR
worn to his shoulders, Jim Casper was in
preventive maintenance and thus didn't see much of Ricardo
Esperanza during work hours, but they had become friends of
a sort. Casper had endured more grumbling about Ricardo's
former wife than he cared to remember.

"Ricardo, you've got to move on. Get someone new."

Ricardo just looked at him. It was never an easy thing to get
Esperanza to agree to hit a few bars and see what might turn
up. Ricardo drew unattached women like flies, a problem
Casper would love to have. Ricardo just brushed them off,
though, and Casper was there to try to interest them in himself.

"You're a goddamn monk, Ricardo. Why don't we have
some fun?"

Only rarely would Esperanza relent, and then they usually
ended up with a couple of compliant women seeking diversion
in the local sports bars. All that had come to a screeching halt
when Esperanza discovered that his former wife had found
someone new.

"What do you do, follow her around?"

"She's my wife! The mother of my son."

The guy Ricardo meant looked like an old man to Casper.

They got a glimpse of him at the Jamison Inn, where Ricardo had driven to look for him.

"This place got a bar?" Casper asked.

"We're not going in."

"Then what the hell?"

"There he is."

A middle-aged guy had appeared on foot and was approaching the entrance of the inn.

"You're kidding."

"They're always together," Ricardo growled.

"Hey, it's a free country."

Ricardo was from Argentina and wanted to apply the rules of his homeland to northern Indiana. It didn't do any good to explain to him that a divorced woman could go out with anyone she liked. It was one of the freedoms they had fought all those wars to preserve.

"Were you in the service?" Ricardo snapped.

Casper had tried to enlist but hadn't passed the physical—or the so-called intelligence test, matching blocks of wood to recesses in the board supposedly of the same shape. "That's not the point."

The middle-aged guy had gone inside. Ricardo put it in reverse, and they got out of there. For once, he agreed to go to a bar where there was some hope of a little action. They managed to get a couple of stools and settled in. Ricardo was watching the televised games, but Casper was looking around.

"Ricardo!"

A real doll had squeezed between them with a big smile for Ricardo. He looked at her coldly. "Hi, Marjorie."

"Introduce me," Casper said, and was ignored by both of them. It took him five minutes to get Marjorie's attention. "You alone?" he asked her.

Casper had suffered that appraising look too often in the past. Her eyes swept over him, and it was like hearing again the bad news from the recruiting sergeant. She turned back to Ricardo, so Casper sought solace in his beer. He wasn't sorry when she went away. What the hell, he might just as well watch the televised sports events.

When he made a trip to the john, though, Marjorie intercepted him. "You and Ricardo are friends?"

"Who's Ricardo?" he asked, grinning.

"I know his wife. We're friends."

She seemed to be reappraising him, and the verdict was not so bad this time. So he stayed there, talking to her; he could always go to the john.

"Aren't you drinking?" she asked.

"My drink is at the bar."

"You could go get it, you know."

He did, telling Ricardo he had hooked up with someone, no need to go into details. Ricardo just shrugged.

Casper had a couple of beers with Marjorie, and then she complained about the noise of the bar.

"Want to try another place?" He remembered he had come with Ricardo. "You got a car?"

"It's outside."

He told Ricardo he was leaving—not that it broke his Argentine heart, but he couldn't just disappear. Marjorie drove across Main to a bar on the opposite side, one without a zillion

159

television sets. He was explaining to Marjorie that he was in maintenance at Notre Dame.

"You work with Ricardo?"

"He's not on my crew."

Her expression suggested that he had impressed her. It seemed inevitable that they would talk about Ricardo and his former wife. Casper mentioned the middle-aged man.

"I thought he was imaginary."

"How so?"

"Do you know Bernice?" Casper let it go, but she didn't. "She's my friend and all that, but the way she talks, all kinds of men are nuts about her."

"Well, Ricardo is."

"What a waste." She sipped her beer. "I mean wasted effort. She'll never go back to him."

They were both a little woozy when they left the bar. It was something new for Casper, being in the passenger seat with a woman at the wheel.

"I've got a son," she said.

"You married?"

"Would I be with you if I was?"

So he gave her directions to his place. Not that he could ask her in. Not that he dared. When they got there, he put his arm on the back of the seat, and she rolled warmly toward him. Some minutes later she drew back. "It's funny kissing a man with long hair."

"I never tried it."

She dug him in the ribs, and Casper felt like a wit.

The next time, he picked her up and took her where he was

sure Ricardo wouldn't be, but even so all she talked about was Ricardo and his former wife. Still, it wasn't so bad. The two of them seemed to draw closer as she talked of the other couple. Casper was sure that his ship had come in, and he was making plans for the big move.

He still hadn't got around to it when one night she had something she couldn't wait to tell him, "The man found dead on campus the other day? That was the guy Bernice said was nuts about her."

She went on, and when Casper realized what she was suggesting, he came to Ricardo's defense. "He wouldn't do a thing like that." Even as he said it, he thought of how obsessed Ricardo was with the way his ex-wife was playing around.

"I wonder if we ever know who would do what," Marjorie said.

"I know what I would like to do."

And they did it. Later, driving home, Casper thought that his chest expansion had doubled. In bed, he remembered what she had said about Ricardo, and it no longer seemed fantastic. Latin blood and all that. Marjorie really surprised him when she told him she had called the police and told them about Ricardo and the dead man. Geez. Not that she had identified herself, she added.

"Smart."

"The important thing is that they know."

15 WHEN JIMMY STEWART PUT THE question to him, Ricardo Esperanza said he didn't remember what he had been doing on the Sunday night when Xavier Kittock had been killed, or where he had been. He even seemed to have trouble remembering that a dead man had been found on a campus bench.

"He was a friend of your wife."

"She divorced me."

"You take that pretty hard?"

"Wouldn't you?"

Jimmy thought of the wife that had walked out on him. That had stung his pride, but life had actually been better since she left. "Maybe."

"I heard he died of a heart attack."

"Then you do remember."

"Now that you mention it."

"People say you were pretty angry about his friendship with your wife."

"Who?"

"Friends of your wife."

He sniffed. "Marjorie Waters."

The name of the anonymous caller. The wife had thought so, too. "And people who work with you."

Incredulity flickered across Ricardo's handsome face, but then he seemed to remind himself of the perfidy of friends. "Jim Casper. What did he say?"

"And then there was your public threat to Kittock."

"What are you getting at?"

"What do you think?"

Ricardo clammed up. It was just as well. Jimmy didn't want to continue until the guy had a lawyer. "I'll read you your Miranda rights."

"Carmen?"

Jimmy laughed. "How come you remember Carmen Miranda?"

"I saw her movies in Buenos Aires."

That got him talking again, but now it was just about himself, so that was all right. Jimmy was almost sorry for the man when he told him he was taking him in for questioning.

"You are questioning me."

"Ricardo, it looks to me as if you had all the reason in the world to kill Xavier Kittock. You can't say where you were at the time. And we did find the plastic bag."

Jimmy waited, but Ricardo gave no sign that the remark affected him. Now Jimmy wished he had mentioned the plastic bag before he told Ricardo he had to take him in.

———

Hairs from the dead man had been found inside the plastic bag. The only clear prints on it turned out to be the space cadet's—Larry Douglas—and the victim's.

"Are you saying he snuffed himself?"

"I'm telling you what we found on the bag." Pincer from the lab sounded huffy.

"Or that maybe Larry Douglas did it."

Pincer found the suggestion intriguing, and Jimmy rose to leave the lab.

"There were smudged prints around the opening of the bag, nothing clear."

"The kind that would have been made by the one who pulled the bag over his head and strangled him?"

"Strangled him? He could have been just making sure the guy couldn't pull the bag off."

"And had a heart attack?"

"You'll have to ask Feeney about that."

Feeney was morose. His intern, Kimberley, had told him she had decided to leave and continue her education.

"It's not a permanent position, Feeney," Jimmy said.

"I know. And she really didn't like the work. The bodies." He made a face. "I know how she feels."

"Any further thoughts on Xavier Kittock?"

"I had to release the body. The relatives were complaining." Feeney rubbed his bald head as if he were looking for hair. "Even if it was a heart attack, it would have been brought on by the struggle when the plastic bag was pulled over his head."

Ricardo had the build of a tango dancer, but how much strength would it take to keep a plastic bag on someone's head when you were standing behind him and caught him unawares?

"Jankowski will get you another intern."

"Jankowski! I wish I could get out of here myself."

Jimmy knew the story about Feeney senior and the water-works. Well, what real difference did it make where Feeney plied his grisly trade?

"Cheer up," Jimmy advised him. "We'll have more bodies for you before long."

Reporters were waiting for Jimmy at his office, and he submitted himself to their questioning.

"It's all pretty circumstantial, isn't it?" Mike Lettney asked. He had wanted to talk to Jimmy in the hall where his cameraman was, but Jimmy had seen himself on television too much to agree to that. Cora Loquitur of what she liked to refer to as the print media had approved of having the interview in Jimmy's office away from the cameras. She wasn't all that photogenic herself.

"Fingerprints aren't circumstantial evidence."

This remark excited Cora, who was used to making logical leaps. Let her speculate, Jimmy thought. It would anger Maple, the lawyer who had taken on Esperanza. Maple was worse than a reporter.

"It's pretty obvious, isn't it, Stewart? Sock it to an immigrant," Maple had said when he arrived at the interrogation room.

"*Cómo?*"

"Funny."

Maple fancied himself the champion of minorities. Jimmy told him that Ricardo hadn't come in across the Rio Grande. "He flew in from Buenos Aires. His father is a professor there."

"You sound like you resent that."

"Not if he doesn't."

Jimmy got rid of the reporters and beat it out of the office so he wouldn't be there when Maple called asking what the hell fingerprints he was telling the press about. In the car he gave Phil Knight a call, and they arranged to meet at the driving range.

16 BECAUSE OF THE DELAY IN RE-
leasing the body of Xavier Kittock, the
relatives and friends who had come to campus for his funeral
had a prolonged visit. This proved to be a bonus for Roger
Knight, who was able to have a number of extended conversations with the interesting father of Rebecca de Vega Nobile.

"Her mother was at best tolerant of that middle name,"
David Nobile said with a smile. "But then, Rebecca was her
own mother's name, and that gained her assent."

"Quid pro quo."

"Exactly. But tell me about the edition you ordered through
Boris Henry."

Phil slipped discreetly from the room to the solace of the
television while Roger brought out the recent acquisition and
handed it to his guest. For an hour the two men examined the
prize.

"I wonder if he has other things," Nobile murmured.

"We can find out." Roger wheeled to his computer and
brought up the Web site of Boris Henry Rare Books.

While this feast of reason went on, Mrs. Nobile and her
daughter were enjoying one another's company whenever Rebecca was not in class. With maternal wariness, Mrs. Nobile

had met Josh Daley and wondered what this new friendship portended.

"We have a class together. And we run."

"Run?"

Rebecca explained. It all sounded wholesome enough. Mrs. Nobile was torn between the desire that her daughter should graduate and emerge into the wider world still single and the equally strong desire that she might meet the companion of her life here on campus. Was Josh Daley that companion? It was clear to her that the young man didn't have the mind of her daughter, nor share Rebecca's interests, but then there are so many facets to a life together, as she had learned. David's bibliophilic bent had not been evident during the years when her husband had amassed the wealth that had brought him leisure enough in midlife to pursue his surprising interest in the golden age of Spanish literature. Rebecca was her father's child, and Mrs. Nobile began to weigh the possibility that Josh might be the complement to her daughter that she herself was for her husband. Such thoughts distracted her from the grief she felt at her brother's death.

The realization that Xavier's death had not been natural added to the horror. When the young man employed in campus maintenance was arrested under suspicion of having killed Xavier, Mrs. Nobile took to her room in the Morris Inn, inconsolable in grief.

"It's better for her to be alone just now," Rebecca said, as she and Josh prepared for their run. With practice, her endurance had increased, and she found it oddly pleasant to run in relative silence at Josh's side.

The route they took had become a familiar one, around both lakes and then from the Grotto along the road to St. Mary's and back again. This was far shorter than the distance Josh was used to, but he did not want to push her beyond her present strength. They ended on a bench beside a campus walk that led to Old College, the most ancient campus building. It overlooked the lake.

"My father is with Roger Knight, They're asking him to help fund the Zahm Center."

Josh was now regularly auditing Roger's class devoted to John Zahm, a pleasant relief from Continental epistemology. "It's odd that both your uncle and Boris Henry developed such an interest in Zahm."

"Not only them. Paul Lohman is another. They all roomed together. The Three Musketeers."

Paul Lohman had arrived from Chicago, where he had been on business. Rebecca and her parents had dined with him, Boris Henry, and the elegant Clare Healy. Lohman was a short, cheery man who relieved what might have been the lugubrious atmosphere at their table with a lengthy account of the Red Sox's prospects for the season. Boris Henry seemed to regret the loss of the Zahm diary as much as he did his old roommate.

"Is there only the one copy?" Paul Lohman asked.

"It was never published. Of course there is only the one copy."

"You should have photocopied it."

Boris Henry stared at him. "Have you any idea what such an item is worth? It is as fragile as it is valuable. You don't subject a thing like that to a Xerox machine."

"You might have made a longhand copy, then."

"I intend to get it back! I have hired Philip Knight for that purpose."

"Roger Knight's brother?" David Nobile's interest had finally been engaged.

"He is a private investigator."

"I had no idea."

"He only takes on very special projects these days."

"I'm sure he will find it," Clare Healy said.

Boris Henry reacted to this with impatience. "Clare, I needn't tell you of the shadier aspects of the rare book trade. God knows where the thing might have been spirited off to."

"I'm sure he does," Mrs. Nobile said. Her loss had brought on a bout of piety. "Have you all been to the Grotto?"

"Not yet," Paul Lohman said.

"Tell me about it," Clare urged, and Mrs. Nobile was only too happy to oblige. The replica of the shrine at Lourdes was a token of Father Edward Sorin's devotion to the Virgin Mary, the name of the university he had founded being another.

"You must take me there, Boris," Clare Healy said.

Rebecca could not figure out the relationship between Boris Henry and this woman with the patrician air whom he had described as the effective manager of his rare book business. How so serene a woman could radiate such femininity was a marvel.

"Has Philip Knight turned up anything yet?" Paul asked.

170

Boris shook his head.

"I suppose the police are involved as well."

"No! Good Lord, the less publicity the better. You realize that everything I have said is confidential."

They all realized it. Paul Lohman twisted an imaginary key in his lips and tossed it over his shoulder, getting a laugh from Clare, but immediately afterward, he was talking again. "Didn't Eggs join an expedition in search of sunken treasure?"

"Sunken treasure!" David Nobile perked up, and the story was told, Boris and Clare spelling one another.

"That was the basis of his interest in Zahm," Boris concluded, and began to talk about Father Zahm's South American travels and his interest in El Dorado.

Rebecca tuned him out. Who could compete with Roger Knight on the subject of Father Zahm? Knight's course, spurred by recent events, had veered into a discussion of Father Zahm's travel writings, interrupting his account of the priest's interest in Dante. The subject had taken him far afield, leading to a long and fascinating hour on the subject of rare metals.

"Gold has practical uses, of course," Roger said to his class. "And not merely dental. But it is its comparative rarity, and, of course, its beauty, that explains the fascination it has always had. Mere rarity would not be enough, would it? And yet one thinks of the bars of gold bullion sleeping unused and highly protected at Fort Knox, Kentucky. They are still there even though the gold standard is a thing of the past. Once paper currency had been an implicit claim on that treasure, but no more. I find that there is a brisk trade in gold, quite independent of money and stocks and bonds." He grew more pensive. "But its value is expressed in dollars."

There was a ruminative, almost melancholy tone to his voice, and Rebecca commented on it.

Roger smiled. "I am mimicking Father Zahm's tone as he wrote of such things. Who has read *Treasure Island*?"

Josh, of course. The class had ended with Roger and Josh exchanging delighted memories of the novel.

Thinking of this, sitting beside Josh on a bench overlooking the lake, deliciously tired, Rebecca, said, "For a history major, you certainly know a lot of things."

"Not epistemology."

"Epistemology isn't everything."

His hand found hers, and they sat on in silence.

"I HAVEN'T SAT ON A BENCH SINCE this happened," Armitage Shanks said with what might have been a shudder—but then, he shook all the time.

"Have you stopped sending your shirts out?"

"I always have them back on hangers."

The Old Bastards were at lunch at their table in the University Club, happy to have the new twists in the death of Xavier Kittock to enliven their day.

"I got out my records," Goucher said. "I never had him in class."

"The maintenance man?"

"Kittock."

"Class of '74."

"You've been reading the *Observer*." A low growl went around the round table, and the conversation threatened to get diverted onto the topic of the student newspaper.

"What was the motive?" Shanks asked querulously.

"A jealous husband," Debbie, the hostess, said, sitting on the edge of an unclaimed chair.

"Chaucer."

"No, Esperanza."

"When's the funeral?"

Here was a lugubrious topic they could all get their teeth into, artificial or not. They had all long been in that twilit time of life when the daily obituaries are the first items read in the newspaper. Their companions had been picked off one by one, and they had taken pews in Sacred Heart to bid them a last adieu and ponder their own fate. To a man, they had plots awaiting them in Cedar Grove. Shanks, a bachelor, had already put up a marker over his: name, date of birth, and then a blank awaiting the day when the bell would toll for him. He had wrung a promise from the others that "Notre Dame Our Mother" would not be sung as taps at his obsequies.

"What's the difference? You won't hear it."

"It's a tearjerker!"

"How about the *Salve Regina?*" This beautiful hymn was sung over the grave of a newly buried member of the Congregation of Holy Cross, but that was in the community cemetery. The Old Bastards never missed a funeral there, watching an old adversary being lowered into the ground.

"You're all too mean to die," Debbie said. She had taken some plastic-wrapped crackers from the bowl in the middle of the table and turned them in her hand as if contemplating a bet.

"No one means to die," Armitage Shanks said primly. "It is an end, not an aim." He looked around brightly as once he had looked when he taught philosophy.

"A jealous husband, Debbie?"

At first she thought the question was personal. It took a while to pick up the broken rhythm of conversation at this table.

"The dead man had become interested in Esperanza's former wife. He threatened him in front of witnesses," she explained.

"What kind of name is Esperanza?"

"A noun."

"It means hope." Armitage Shanks again.

"The wife seems to want to hang him," Debbie said.

"How so?"

"She's been babbling to the press about her husband's insane jealousy."

"Marriage as temporary insanity."

"Everything's temporary."

A gloomy pause. Rush began to speak on the nature of time. The past is no more, the future is not yet, the present is merely the division between them, so what is time?

Armitage Shanks looked at his watch and answered the question.

Debbie rose. "Who wants another drink?"

"On the house?"

"Oh, you can have it right here."

Off she went, stirring distant memories in old bodies, as Goucher recited Whitman. *Out of the cradle, endlessly rocking . . .*

18 - - - - - - ⟶ PAUL LOHMAN'S FIRM WAS LO-
cated in Chicago, but he had kept the
books for Boris Henry's business as well as his personal finances during all the years since Henry had been left a widower. This made him privy to many things in his old
roommate's personal life that he suspected not even Clare
Healy knew. It was because of Clare that Paul's visits to
Kansas City had become a labor of love. Thanks to her, Henry
Rare Books was a solid money earner—nothing dramatic, not
enough to bail Boris out of his gambling debts, but sequestered, thanks to Paul, from Boris's personal finances so
that, in the event of a crash, it would float free as an eventual
life raft. When Paul had made these arrangements, he had
been thinking only of Boris, but over time he came to see it as
a favor he had done for Clare.

Had she any inkling of the madness that gripped Boris when
he entered a casino? The spread of gambling opportunities
across the nation increased temptation exponentially for one
with Boris's proclivities. Once one had to go off to the fleshpots
of Las Vegas, and then New Jersey, but now the rivers of the
nation harbored gambling boats and the shores of the Great
Lakes were dotted with them. Even in the wilderness a glitzy

building emerged from a background of primeval forest, a casino run by a local tribe of Indians. It was not a matter of being led into temptation but of needing to be led out of it.

Of course, concupiscence, an all but universal weakness, was addressed constantly by advertising, fashion, and music, if you could stand it, but there was a natural limit to such vice, whereas gambling was halted only when one's money had been exhausted. Perhaps there was an analogy there.

At table in the Morris Inn, with the Nobiles and their lovely daughter, Boris, and Clare, Paul had marveled at the facade Boris showed the world. Portrait of a rare book dealer whose mind was ever on transcendent and lasting things. He had fashioned a business that enabled him to combine the keen pleasure he had in learning with a nice return on his investment.

David Nobile clearly envied him. "What better life could there be?" he said, sighing.

"That of a professor," Rebecca said firmly.

"Please don't get started on Roger Knight," her mother pleaded.

David Nobile nodded to his daughter. "You're right. But what Boris does comes right after it."

Paul Lohman's eyes met Clare's across the table. The expression in hers was uncommunicative, but he suspected that she was contrasting this public portrait of Boris with his hectic private life.

From the restaurant, after bidding Rebecca good night, they drifted into the bar. As he turned from the bar with his drink, Paul saw Clare holding a long-stemmed glass of wine, moving away. He followed her to where she stood looking out at the courtyard.

Paul pushed the door open. "Let's get a little air."

Her serene eyes were briefly on him. She nodded and went outside.

There were tables there, and an odd sort of privacy. Through the windows of the restaurant and bar they could see diners and drinkers but were invisible to them. Clare sighed.

"A sad business," he said.

"I have to remind myself that he was your roommate."

"And Boris's. You must have met him."

"Oh, yes."

"There was always competition between Eggs and Boris."

"Competition?"

"I mean long ago." Had she thought he was referring to her?

"Paul, do you know what I would really like to do?"

"What?"

"See the Grotto. Is it far?"

"A pretty long walk."

"I have a car."

"Let's go."

They left their drinks on the metal table and went inside, passing the open door of the bar. When they emerged on the opposite side of the inn, Paul realized he had been holding his breath, fearful that someone would see them and call out. Of course, it was ridiculous to think of this otherwise than as what it was, a visit to the Grotto, no one's idea of a rendezvous. Even so, as she drove, following his directions, he was suddenly conscious of his life. Returning to Notre Dame always brought memories, of course, but it was here that Paul had fallen in love and failed to win the girl. His reaction had been to throw himself into his work. He flattered himself that he had done better financially than either of his roommates, but suddenly that seemed hollow. What an odd trio they were, the Three Musketeers. None of them had a family; Eggs had never had a wife, either, and Boris's marriage had been tragically brief. The death of his wife had left him rich, but he had frittered the money away on the stupidest habit in the world.

"Where can I park?"

"Anywhere. Campus security won't bother a visitor to the Grotto." He picked a briefcase up off the floor and was about to put it in the backseat.

"Is that your briefcase?" she asked.

"Mine?"

"It must be Boris's. Let me see."

He gave it to her, and she snapped it open. "It's his," she said, looking inside. She was closing the top when she stopped and opened it again. She took from it a plastic bag.

Light from a streetlamp illuminated the inside of the car. She held the bag up. It was the kind used to store things in a freezer. "For heaven's sake. Why would he have his wallet in his briefcase?" She slid the bag open and brought forth a wallet. After she opened it, she turned toward Paul, her face in shadow now.

"What is it?" She handed it to him. He held the wallet for a moment, then opened it as she had. "My God."

The wallet belonged to Xavier Kittock. His keys and other items were also in the bag.

PART THREE

THE GOLDEN RULE

1   HAVING PUT THE PLASTIC BAG
filled with Eggs's effects back into the
briefcase, Clare snapped it shut. After she locked the car, she
and Paul Lohman went on to the Grotto, where they sat on a
bench and stared at the flickering votive candles. Beyond an
initial expression of surprise, neither of them had said anything.

"There has to be an explanation," Clare murmured now.

"Of course."

Eggs's pockets had been empty when he was found, and
what had been in his pockets was in a bag in Boris's briefcase.
It was difficult for Paul to see what innocent explanation of
that could be found.

"Someone must have put them in his briefcase, Paul. After
all, it wasn't locked."

"Who?"

"Whoever killed poor Eggs." Clare's thoughts seemed to be
racing. "And it could have been anytime, anywhere. He left the
briefcase in the car—we had gone several places together—
but before that, it would have been in his room."

"They think that maintenance man, Esperanza, killed
him."

Clare turned to him suddenly. "Paul, I think I know what happened."

"What?"

"One of the places Boris and I went was to Eggs's room. As soon as I arrived from Kansas City. It was two in the morning, and we went to the Jamison Inn, and they let us in. We went there to look for the diary. Boris was sure Eggs had stolen it."

"But you didn't find it."

"No. Look, I was in the bathroom, looking around. I think Boris must have found that bag and taken it then."

"Clare, you realize that doesn't make sense. Why would the stuff from Eggs's pockets be in a plastic bag in his own room?"

She stared at him as her explanation crumbled. She turned away. "I don't know."

"The question is, what are we going to do?"

"Paul, we have to keep it quiet!"

A tempting course of action. What Paul really wished was that they had not found that bag. Now they faced a terrible dilemma. If they kept quiet about it, they would reinforce the case against Esperanza. But what if he were innocent?

"I'm going to talk to Boris," he said.

"Oh my God."

"Clare, it's the only way. If there is an explanation, he can provide it."

She fell silent, then said in a small voice, "And if he can't?"

"What possible motive could he have for killing Eggs?"

She gasped when he said it so bluntly. "That's the problem."

"You'd better tell me everything."

"Why do you suppose Eggs was on campus in the first place?"

Paul listened to her account of Eggs and Boris talking in Kansas City about the Zahm diary and about South American gold and El Dorado. Eggs had already been bitten by the bug of lost treasure; he had invested in and gone on an expedition that had hoped to locate a Spanish galleon, loaded with gold on its homeward voyage, sunk off the coast of South America. "Boris was positive that the diary provided accurate information on the location of El Dorado. He must have convinced Eggs," she concluded.

"Did Boris show him the diary?"

"No. That's why Eggs must have hoped that Zahm's letters of the period might contain whatever information was in the diary."

"Did he show you the diary?"

"Paul, I have to tell you that, apart from the diary's historical importance, and the interest it would have for Notre Dame or others connected with the university, I was sure that all this talk about El Dorado was nonsense."

"So you didn't see the diary?"

"Oh, I saw it. It's real. But he wouldn't even let me read it. And he stashed it in his safe-deposit box in the bank until he brought it here, even though we have a vault in the store."

"And while he was here, the diary was stolen?"

"That's what he said."

"Don't you believe him?"

"Paul, he had high hopes for that diary. He was sure the

185

university would make a handsome bid for it. Its being stolen would have enhanced its value and spurred more interest."

"Quite a gamble."

She looked at him. "I know all about that, Paul."

That saved him having to tell her that her boss was a compulsive gambler. "You two were very close, I suppose."

"Not like that."

The words seemed to drift toward the Grotto and mingle with the wisps of smoke rising from the votive candles. Paul found that he was elated by her remark. "I wish there were someone I could talk to about this." He fell silent. "A priest."

"There are plenty of them here."

"I've got it. Father Carmody. He called me recently about contributing to the founding of a Zahm Center."

"That was Boris's idea. I mean the center."

"So I can talk with him about that and hope for an opportunity to bring up our dilemma."

Our dilemma. At table earlier, struck as always by Clare's cool beauty, he had wondered what miracle could bring them together. Nonetheless, lovely as she was, and no matter how close this puzzle had drawn them, Paul would give it all up in return for not having found that plastic bag in Boris's briefcase.

2   FATHER CARMODY WAS STILL AT
breakfast when Paul Lohman came to
see him at the Holy Cross retirement house. It was not yet
eight o'clock, and the priest had timed his breakfast so that he
would have fasted for at least an hour before saying the funeral Mass at Sacred Heart.

"Ah. Are you my ride?"

Paul Lohman seemed surprised at the question, and Father
Carmody explained.

"Of course, Father. I'll be glad to take you to Sacred
Heart."

"Are you going like that?"

"I'll have to change first, of course." Lohman acted as if he
had forgotten about his old roommate's funeral. "Father, I
have to talk to you."

The old priest felt a tremor of premonition. In the nature of
things, he had become reconciled to the violent death of
Xavier Kittock on campus. Dreadful things have a way of being domesticated by the passage of time. But Lohman's manner suggested that more bad news was in the offing. He
pushed back from the table, then did not rise.

"Would you like some breakfast?"

"No. Thank you. I can get something later."

The priest rose then and took Lohman outside to the patio, where they sat on chairs facing the lake, with the golden dome and the spire of Sacred Heart Basilica visible above the trees. Lohman began immediately. Listening to him, Father Carmody felt the weight of this new information pressing on him. When the story was told, they sat in silence for a moment.

"Who have you told?"

"I wanted to see you first."

"That was wise. Now I know. I will take it from here."

Lohman actually slumped in his chair with relief. "There must be an explanation, Father."

"No doubt. And I will find out what it is. In the meantime, there is no need for you to tell this story to others."

"Of course not. Father, the three of us were roommates."

Father Carmody took the point. It was on the face of it absurd that these events were explained by the falling-out of old friends. Notre Dame alumni did not fall out. This article of Father Carmody's creed was easier to state than to apply to Boris Henry.

"And the lady, Clare Healy? She must trust me, too."

"She will be as relieved as I am that you're taking responsibility in the matter."

"Good," Father Carmody said. "But just to make certain, you might specifically enjoin her to silence." No need to add that a woman might find silence more difficult than a man.

"Do you think I should talk to Boris?"

"No need for that. You run along now and get some breakfast and change. I can get to Sacred Heart all right."

188

Lohman left like one released from a great burden, and, watching him lope away, Father Carmody once more felt a massive weight on his shoulders. A weight that he intended to share with Philip Knight.

Curious students and faculty, plus prurient townies drawn by the insinuating accounts in the local newspaper, made the funeral of Xavier Kittock a well-attended event, but Father Carmody addressed his remarks to the mourners in the front pew. Natural death is shock enough, but to bury one whose death was due to violence calls upon the deepest resources of the homilist. Mrs. Nobile, sister of the deceased, was the closest blood relative, and she wept silently, bracketed by her husband and daughter. Boris Henry and Paul Lohman were on either side of a woman who must be Clare Healy.

The old priest went lightly on the grim stakes of life but avoided suggesting that even now Xavier Kittock was enjoying the beatific vision, no longer vulnerable to the slings and arrows of outrageous fortune. It occurred to Father Carmody that the devotees of Father Zahm who sat before him must know of that priest's interest in Dante. How in the modern world had the Florentine's robust faith in the great either/or of the next world survived? So Father Carmody consoled the mourners but did not canonize the departed. Afterward, the friends and family came along to Cedar Grove, where a plot had been found for the slain alumnus.

"This used to be the sixteenth fairway," Father Carmody said, as he and Philip Knight walked away from the grave site.

"The final divot?"

"Ho ho. You have a car?"

Phil pointed.

"Good. I'll say a last word to these folks and be with you in a jiffy."

While he spoke with Mrs. Nobile, her husband took the priest's hand and pressed something into it.

"What's this?"

"With our gratitude, Father."

The glimpse Father Carmody took revealed a denomination he had never before seen on the legal tender of the nation.

"That's not necessary."

"All the more deserving, then."

Well, well. Father Carmody put the money into his pocket. Secular clergy were used to stipends and gifts on such occasions, he supposed, but he was not.

Boris Henry came up to him. "You gave Kittock a perfect send-off, Father."

In the light of what he had learned a few hours earlier, Father Carmody found the remark freighted with ambiguity. Henry's gaze seemed untroubled, but Father Carmody had long since realized that the guilty do not often wear their sins upon their faces.

"I wonder who of us will be next?" Father Carmody sighed.

Boris Henry stepped back in surprise. "Not me, I hope."

"More likely myself. Well, I am off."

Philip Knight stood beside his car, gazing westward. "Was that the sixteenth green?"

"It was. This was the longest hole on the course, a par five. I was always happy to get a bogie."

Now a fence separated the expanded cemetery from the remainder of the fairway and the green beyond.

"It's odd, a golf course becoming a cemetery," Phil said.

Father Carmody had opposed halving the old course to accommodate residence halls and the cemetery, but he must not be tempted along that path of resentment. He was anxious to tell Philip Knight what he had learned from Paul Lohman. Not that he thought that even Phil would be able to cushion the university from further bad publicity.

3 BERNICE HAD THOUGHT SERI-
ously about attending Xavier Kittock's
funeral but reluctantly decided not to, mainly because Marjorie had thought it a good idea.

"You'd wear a veil, of course. It wouldn't do to be recognized."

Then what was the point of going? Bernice imagined people looking at her, whispering to one another, fascinated by the tragic woman who had come to mourn her husband's victim.

"Ricardo would kill me."

"How could he?"

They stopped at the dry cleaner's to pick up things Bernice should have claimed weeks ago. Marjorie professed to be moved by the sight of Ricardo's clothes—his good suit and some dress shirts.

"You send his laundry to the dry cleaner?"

Bernice just looked at her. Throwing things of little Henry's into the washer was one thing, but she was not going to be Ricardo's washerwoman. In any case, these clothes were the second batch of things he hadn't taken with him when he moved out, and she hadn't wanted to send him a bag of dirty laundry. The shirts were individually wrapped and then enclosed in a larger plastic bag.

"Let's have lunch," Marjorie suggested.

Marjorie was back in the role of best friend, come to Bernice's side in her time of misfortune. How many women had a husband accused of murder? Bernice hadn't gone to work since Ricardo had been arrested. She reminded Marjorie that Ricardo was her *former* husband.

"Oh, I know that, all right."

"What do you mean?"

"Good Lord, you're not going to be jealous, are you?"

"Jealous of what?"

"As you said, he's your former husband."

Bernice would have liked to laugh at the hint that Ricardo had been chasing after Marjorie, but she found she was angry. If he had to see other women, why would he pick Marjorie Waters? The answer to that seemed suddenly clear. It was Marjorie who picked him.

"I don't want to have lunch."

"Bernice, you have to eat."

"I have errands. Where should I drop you?"

"I told you. I'm at your disposal." She made it sound like the thing in the kitchen sink.

Marjorie seemed almost to be enjoying the drama in which Bernice found herself. Bernice wanted to free herself of this suffocating sympathy. She headed for Marjorie's apartment and came to a stop before it.

"Bernice, I mean it. You really shouldn't be alone."

"I'll call you."

Marjorie had no choice, but she took her time getting out of the car. When she went to her door, she put a lot of rhythm into her walk.

Finding a parking place downtown within walking distance of the County Building was no easy matter even though the once thriving center of the city had been depleted by the transfer to the malls of department stores and boutiques and just about everything else but banks. Bernice finally found a spot near the College Football Hall of Fame and walked three blocks to the County Building. Inside, she had to go through a metal detector, but that gave her time to ask the security woman where the jail was.

Trousered and in shirt and tie, poured into the outfit, the woman looked at her with faint curiosity. "Take the elevator."

Upstairs, Bernice identified herself as Ricardo's wife and asked if she could see him. She was taken off to a room empty save for a table and several uncomfortable chairs. A clock on the wall moved so imperceptibly you would have thought that the earth was slowing down in its passage around the sun. After ten minutes, a door opened, and there was Ricardo.

He stopped after coming into the room and looked at her. "They said my wife was here."

"Oh, Ricardo."

Then, incredibly, she was in his arms. All her discontents seemed to evaporate, not least because she imagined Marjorie seeing this tender scene.

"How's Henry?"

"Fine."

"Does he know I'm here?"

"Ricardo, he wouldn't understand if I told him."

"Don't tell him. They're going to have to let me go."

"Of course they are!" The thought that Ricardo could have killed X was silly. They sat side by side at the table.

"Do you have a lawyer?"

"I won't need one now."

"Why?"

"The police have found something. I should have been let go hours ago."

4   PAUL LOHMAN TOLD FATHER CAR-
mody, and Father Carmody told Phil
Keegan, and Phil brought the news to Jimmy Stewart.

"Where is it?"

"In Boris Henry's briefcase."

"And where the hell is that?"

"I thought you'd want to talk to Henry when you go out
there to get the briefcase."

"Good God, Phil, he could have gotten rid of that bag."

"Lohman is keeping an eye on him."

Jimmy didn't like it, and Phil didn't blame him. On the
other hand, he understood why Lohman and Clare Healy had
been reluctant to be any more directly involved than they already were in what was about to befall Boris Henry. The drive
to campus was largely silent until Jimmy said, "I never
thought Ricardo was guilty."

"What's he like?"

"You're thinking immigrant? Forget it. It turns out he is a
very educated man, no matter his current employment."

"The wife doesn't suggest that."

Jimmy nodded. "She seemed almost ashamed of him, didn't
she?"

"How's his English?"

"As good as yours."

"That bad?"

So they were once again on easy terms when Jimmy turned into the parking lot of the Morris Inn. Before they went in, Phil led Jimmy to the rental car Clare Healy had driven from Chicago. The briefcase was still visible through the window.

Boris Henry was in the bar with Paul Lohman and Clare Healy, and there was no apprehension in his manner as the two men approached the table. Paul pushed his chair back, and Clare did the same.

"Boris," Phil said. "We'd like to talk to you alone."

Boris looked excited. "Have you found it?"

"Clare and I will skeddadle," Lohman said, avoiding everyone's eyes.

"What's the secret? Stick around, you can hear this."

Stewart indicated to the others that they should go. Boris hunched forward at the table, accepting that he was to get the news solo. His manner seemed to suggest he now thought that was just as well.

Jimmy said, "Mr. Henry, why are you trying to fool my good friend Phil Knight?"

"Fool him?" Boris tried frowning. He tried a laugh. Finally he just looked at Jimmy.

"I think you still have that diary."

"Why the hell would you think that?" Henry turned to Phil. They were all seated now. "What is this, Phil?"

197

"It has been suggested to the police that you have what we're looking for in your briefcase."

Boris shook his head. "Do you think I would fake the theft of Father Zahm's diary?" His tone suggested this would have been akin to sacrilege. Suddenly, he looked hard at Jimmy. "Who told you such a thing?"

"Where is your briefcase?"

"Now, look here—"

"Boris, if the information is false, that can be established easily. Get your briefcase."

Boris considered this. It was pretty clear he was as disgusted with Phil as he was with Jimmy Stewart. He got to his feet. "Come on."

They followed him out of the bar and up the stairs to the second floor. A cleaning cart was in the hallway near an open door. Boris's room. They walked in, startling the maid.

"We'll just be a minute," Boris told her. He stood by the bed and looked around the room. Of course, the briefcase wasn't there. His face screwed into thought. "It's not here."

"Where might it be?"

"I'm thinking, I'm thinking."

It was like a parlor game, with everyone but Boris knowing the answer. Eventually, he had it. "I think it may be in the car."

"And where is that?"

"Clare has the key."

"We can get it from her."

"What a goddamn wild goose chase," Boris muttered, and led the way out of the room.

Clare was in the lobby, waiting as if by agreement. She came with them into the parking lot, where she unlocked the car and stepped aside.

Boris looked in and then reached for and brought out the briefcase. He put it on the hood of the car. "We can do this right here." He snapped the catches, and the lid opened slowly, as if to reveal dramatically the plastic bag. Boris just pushed it aside, to display what else the briefcase contained. He turned triumphantly. "So much for this nonsense."

Jimmy had taken the plastic bag from the briefcase.

"What's this?"

Boris scarcely glanced at the bag when Jimmy held it up. Jimmy turned the bag slowly. "This your wallet?"

"Wallet?"

"And keys. Change. Handkerchief."

"Let me see that."

Jimmy prevented Boris from grabbing the bag. He slid the top of it open and took out the wallet. It opened in the palm of his hand. He turned to Boris. "Xavier Kittock."

"Come on."

"That's my line, Henry," Jimmy said. "We can continue this downtown."

For a minute, Boris looked as if he might take a swing at Jimmy, but then an icy calm came over him. He turned to Clare. "Call my lawyer in Kansas City and ask him to get the hell up here as fast as he can. Tell him the problem."

5 LARRY DOUGLAS HAD RETURNED to the headquarters of campus security, his workday complete, when he heard his name called. He turned, and there was Kimberley in shorts and halter, a sweatband holding back her hair, pulling a wheeled golf bag.

"I do like that uniform," she cried, delighted. Thank God, he had taken off his stupid helmet before turning around. "Is the gun loaded?"

"Famous last words. You've been golfing."

"Nine holes."

"Alone?"

"No, I played with a couple of strangers. It's so good to be out in the sun and away from that dreadful morgue." She inhaled deeply of the unrefrigerated air.

"You quit?"

Kimberley stood there, the picture of health, slim and beautiful, her face flushed from exercise. "Feeney said he would consider me on leave, but I'm not going back."

"What will you do?"

"Golf?" She smiled with radiant insouciance. "Do you golf?"

"Not much lately. I golfed that course a lot when I was a

kid. I used to go over the fence early in the morning and get in half a dozen holes before the ranger was out."

"When are you through?"

"I'm about to check out."

She waited, her air receptive, inviting poetic thoughts. When he said nothing, she laughed. "I'll wait."

"It'll just be a minute."

Before he got to the door, Laura came out. Had she ever looked fatter? The two women exchanged a glance, and there was immediately enmity between them. Larry slipped inside.

Laura and Kimberley were facing one another when he came out. Before and After. Larry felt like a traitor, but his heart thumped when he looked at Kimberley. He would have given anything to erase the memory of those lengthy evenings in his car when he had grappled with Laura.

Kimberley was describing her job in the morgue as if she hadn't decided to quit. "Larry has seen the place."

"Really?" Laura looked at Larry as if she would like to see him on a slab down there.

Since they all three had cars, the scene dissolved without any need for Larry to explain to Laura who this Diana of the golf course was, this nymph who spoke so matter-of-factly about autopsies. They walked together to their cars, and Larry resisted Laura's efforts to get him aside. He got behind the wheel of his car and started the motor and backed out. He had just turned onto Angela when a horn behind him tooted. He looked into the rearview mirror, expecting to see Laura following him, but it was Kimberley!

He pulled onto a side street and parked, and Kimberley

stopped just behind him. Larry jumped out of his car and went back to her. The thought of asking her into his own car was impossible. Maybe he would get a new car.

"Who's Laura?" Kimberley asked when he got into the passenger seat.

"I thought she was your friend."

"Enemy would be more like it."

"She's in campus security."

"That explains the uniform."

"We could go out 31 and have a beer."

"What about your car?"

"Maybe someone will steal it."

She drove north across the Michigan line, and they stopped at a little A-frame roadhouse and ordered schooners. When they clicked their glasses, Kimberley said, "Here's to campus security."

He would never have dreamed that Laura would fill the role of object of jealousy, let alone with someone like Kimberley. They soon exhausted that subject, Larry adopting the air of the gentleman who never tells.

"There's a lot of excitement downtown," Kimberley said. "You know the body they found on campus?"

"I found it," Larry said.

"Tell me about it."

He did, giving her a version Crenshaw would not have liked to hear. He told her of finding in a trash can the plastic bag that might have been the murder weapon, and he told her that the pockets of the dead man had been empty.

"That explains it, then."

"What do you mean?"

"They found his wallet and keys and things and arrested the man who had them. Boris Henry?"

For a fleeting moment, Larry felt that Kimberley was encroaching on his territory and resented it. From the beginning, he had thought of the Kittock case as his own.

"I always wondered about that guy," he said. Her expression made up for having heard this news from her. "I'll tell you one thing," he went on, "It's a lot easier to work with the South Bend cops than with colleagues in campus security."

She actually put her hand on his. They ordered a second schooner, and Larry began to talk about W. H. Auden.

6 WHEN RICARDO WAS RELEASED, he came to stay with Bernice, saying it was okay, they were still married, the divorce didn't mean a thing.

"So why were you fooling around with Marjorie Waters?"

"Did she say that?"

"Were you?"

"Look, I fought her off."

Bernice beamed. "I can believe it."

Little Henry was not as surprised to have his father in the house as Bernice would have thought. The separation and divorce now seemed almost like a fantastic interlude. She tried to explain it to Marjorie.

"Is that why you talked about him the way you did?"

"Marjorie, you don't understand what it is to be in love."

Marjorie turned away in anger. Over her shoulder, she said, "You're still divorced."

"Tell it to Ricardo. He's always been off-limits, Marjorie."

"What is that supposed to mean?"

"Let's let bygones be bygones. Maybe Ricardo can fix you up with someone on maintenance."

It turned out that the only way they could put the divorce

behind them was by remarrying, and Ricardo refused. "We are married!"

"Not civilly."

"Then we'll just live together uncivilly."

The prospect was almost racy, thought of like that, and Bernice agreed, not that she had any choice. Ricardo couldn't get over the fact that Boris Henry would have let him go on trial for murdering Kittock.

"But you didn't do it."

"Of course I didn't do it. But they arrested me, didn't they?"

"Well, you did threaten him."

"You're damn right I did. Any husband would have."

"Ricardo, there was nothing."

"I know that."

Bernice could take that from him, but she was willing to let Marjorie think that it had been a real affair and that Ricardo had done away with his rival. Even in the altered circumstances, she retained the pleasant thought that she was a woman over whom men fought. And she had gone back to writing, something that annoyed Marjorie more than the suggestion that Bernice was a femme fatale. Ricardo agreed to let her sign up again for the writing course at IUSB now that she had quit her job on campus. Whatever he thought of her writing, it didn't wound his honor the way having a wife working as a waitress had. The novel Bernice was trying to write drew heavily on her own recent experience, and she hinted to Marjorie that the character based on her was sympathetic. Marjorie just stared at her.

Somewhat to Marjorie's surprise, Ricardo did fix her up. It was a double date, and being at the sports bar seemed to take Bernice and Ricardo back to square one. The real surprise was that Marjorie already knew Jim Casper.

"We met right here," Jim said. "One night when Ricardo and I came here."

"I don't remember," Ricardo said.

"You know how those things are," Marjorie said meaningfully. Bernice just smiled. Ricardo had told her all about it.

Casper proposed that they drink to Ricardo's release, and they did, somewhat to Ricardo's annoyance. "Didn't you think I was guilty, Jim?"

"Of what?" Jim tried to dig him in the ribs, but Ricardo was too quick for him.

Perhaps inevitably, they talked about the death of Xavier Kittock. Whenever Bernice tried to get them on another subject, either Casper or Marjorie brought them back to it.

"I'm sure you put the fear of God into him when you threatened him," Marjorie said sweetly.

"I didn't threaten him. I just told him to leave my wife alone."

"Will you remarry?"

"We only marry once in my family. And for keeps."

Bernice squeezed his arm, if only because she knew it would make Marjorie jealous. Jim Casper was okay, although next to Ricardo he looked like an aging hippie.

The perfidy of Boris Henry made Jim almost eloquent. "The bastard would have let you hang for his crime."

Ricardo looked thoughtful. "What an idiot, carrying around the stuff he took from Kittock's pockets."

"I wonder who put the police onto that?" Casper's question gave them all pause.

"Maybe that young guy in campus security. Douglas. The one who found the bag used to smother the guy? He showed more enterprise than the South Bend police," Ricardo said.

"You ought to sue them for false arrest."

"I don't even want to think about it anymore."

7 ROGER KNIGHT AND DAVID NO-
bile sat in Roger's campus office in
Brownson Hall talking about Lope de Vega. Roger had just
put in a call to the Morris Inn and asked Clare Healy if she
were free to talk with some potential customers.

"Haven't you heard what happened? They've arrested
Boris."

"On what basis?"

"Could we meet?"

"In the Morris Inn?"

"I'd rather not."

So Roger gave her directions to his office. Half an
hour later, there was a knock on the door, and David Nobile
got up to answer it. When he opened the door, Clare looked as
if she had come to the wrong place, but then she saw Roger.

"Come in. Come in. There are gods even here. So said Her-
aclitus." Neither of his guests caught the allusion, and Roger
let it go.

When Clare was seated, she looked around the book-filled
room. "Who's the dealer, me or you?"

"Nothing here is for sale. David is especially interested in
Lope de Vega."

"But you just bought a very expensive edition of the poems."

"Don't rub it in," David groaned.

"Have you checked our Web site?"

"Why don't we do that now." Roger turned to his computer and tapped a few keys, and in a moment the handsome page of Henry Rare Books appeared. "Maybe you should do the browsing, Miss Healy."

"Clare."

"Not a Poor Clare, I'm sure." Roger did explain this allusion, and any wit it had was thereby smothered.

Clare settled herself at the computer, and soon Henry's holdings of Lope de Vega appeared. Looking over her shoulder, David was able to determine that there was nothing there he didn't have.

"Then we'll try a wider database." As she tapped the keys, she explained that the holdings of dozens of rare book dealers were entered on a common site. David pulled his chair beside hers and almost immediately cried out. He had spoted the 1621 Madrid edition of *La Filomena*.

"That contains the novella *Las Fortunas de Diana!*"

Roger blinked when he saw what was being asked for this prize, but David Nobile was unfazed. Clare helped him put in an order for the book. When the deed had been done, David showed something of the ambiguous triumph of one whose bid had been accepted at an auction, but satisfaction outweighed any regret at the expenditure.

"Tell me about Boris," Roger said.

The question transformed Clare Healy. Since her arrival

209

she had been the picture of the composed and supremely competent rare book expert. Now her shoulders slumped, and she looked abjectly at Roger. "I still can't believe it."

Beginning slowly, she told the story of her visit to the Grotto with Paul Lohman and their accidental discovery of the contents of Boris's briefcase. "I would give anything if we hadn't opened it."

"Or if Kittock's effects hadn't been in the briefcase."

"Of course."

"Did Boris offer any explanation?"

"His first impulse was to call his lawyer from Kansas City."

"A wise move," David Nobile said.

"Someone could have put those things in his briefcase," Roger said.

"That was my first thought!"

"Did you have a second?"

"I've thought of little else since the police took him away."

"It's odd," Roger said. "There has been a small epidemic of missing things. First, some Father Zahm letters from the archives—"

"That's why Boris and I went to Kittock's room in the Jamison Inn!"

"I don't understand."

"When I arrived from Chicago, it was in the wee hours of the morning, but Boris insisted we had to pay a call on Kittock. He was sure Kittock had taken them."

"Boris Henry was still up when you arrived at the Morris Inn?"

"Sitting in the lobby. I had reached him by my cell phone

to tell him I was on my way. I had no idea he would wait up for me."

"So you went to see Kittock."

"He wasn't in." She paused. "Of course, now we know why."

"And the letters were in his room?"

"Boris found them. I was looking in the bathroom, and he called me out. There they were on the desk."

"Well, they are safely back in the archives now. I wonder where the diary is."

"God only knows."

"You don't suppose that Boris Henry had the letters with him when you went to the Jamison Inn and put them on the desk while you were looking in the bathroom?"

Her mouth opened slowly. "Why on earth would he do a thing like that?"

"I suspect the police will be more interested in learning that he was up and dressed during the time that Kittock met his death."

"Oh my God." Suddenly her old manner was back. "I won't tell them what we did that night." Roger said nothing, nor did David Nobile. "And neither of you must tell them, either."

Roger said softly, "I doubt that either of us will be asked."

"Of course you won't be. There is no reason the police would find out about that visit."

"No. But things look bad enough for Boris as they are."

A grim little smile appeared on her pretty lips. "Foster is a very, very good lawyer."

8   THE OLD BASTARDS, AT THEIR CUS-
tomary table in the University Club,
were reviewing recent events and making mordant comments.

"I always thought Zahm was overestimated."

"By whom?"

"Not by me. Do you know he wrote with great confidence that the earth was no more than ten thousand years old?"

"What difference does it make?"

Cosmo, who had lectured on astronomy, made an impatient sound. "I suppose you find merit in the geocentric system, too?"

"What has Zahm to do with the murder?"

"What has the age of the earth got to do with anything?"

"It's a sad day when one alumnus is accused of murdering another."

"You mean when one roommate is accused of murdering another."

"That sounds like a mitigating circumstance."

"They were roommates?"

"In Zahm."

"Isn't that hall ten thousand years old?"

Debbie paused to refill water glasses. Cosmo said he wanted another drink.

"I thought you were the designated driver."

"The National League doesn't accept that rule. Pitchers hit."

Debbie looked ready to hit him with the water pitcher. "Another Bloody Mary?"

"Another round."

"On you?"

"Of course on me. I am a retired professor in possession of limitless funds. Buy your own drink."

"I would never order or pay for a drink called a Bloody Mary. It is sheer anti-Catholic bigotry."

"I checked my old grade books. I never had either of them in class."

"Are you proposing that as an alibi?"

"Elsewhere."

"What?"

"That's what alibi means."

"You always were a pedant."

"Does knowing the meaning of Latin words make one a pedant?"

"Only when one parades his knowledge."

"Parading knowledge. What an odd phrase."

The new round of drinks arrived, and arthritic hands closed around glasses.

"How did the one roommate murder the other?"

"By pulling a plastic bag over his head and smothering him."

"Ingenious."

"What kind of a plastic bag?"

"The kind shirts come from the laundry in."

"Not strong enough. It would have torn."

"Tell that to the dead man."

"Have you kept all your old grade books?"

"Of course."

"Why? To blackmail former students?"

"I intend to donate them to the archives."

"They can rest there with the grade books of Father Zahm."

"For ten thousand years."

An overweight matron passed their table, enveloped in a cloud of perfume.

"This place is getting to smell like a brothel."

"I defer to your experience of such places."

"You should marry again."

"And honeymoon at Viagra Falls?"

While this was being explained, the waiter brought their separate bills. The Old Bastards bent over them with the eagerness of accountants.

9 ROGER COULD NOT, OF COURSE, keep from Phil what he had learned from Clare Healy. The fact that Boris Henry had been dressed and waiting for Clare in the lobby of the Morris Inn when she arrived from Chicago, added to the discovery of the missing contents of Kittock's pockets in his briefcase, tightened the noose around Boris's neck. The Knight brothers were sitting in on the session, largely because Boris Henry regarded them as allies. He explained to his lawyer that he had engaged Phil to find the missing Zahm diary. Then Jimmy asked Boris where he was during the hours when Xavier Kittock was murdered.

"You don't have to discuss this," Foster said. The Kansas City lawyer gave no sign of his hurried journey to Boris Henry's side. That was where he sat, literally, in the brightly lit interrogation room.

"Why wouldn't I discuss it? I was in the Morris Inn."

"In your room."

"What time are we talking of?"

"I've been told you were seen in the lobby in the wee hours of the morning, dressed."

"It's not likely I'd go down there in my pajamas."

"The time of death has been placed around midnight or slightly after."

"Okay. You say you were told I was in the lobby of the inn."

"At two."

"Before that I was in my room."

Roger said, "Why did you go down to the lobby?"

"Clare called from Chicago when she started out in the rental car."

"What time was that?"

"Eleven, eleven-thirty. She let me know she was leaving Chicago. I suppose it was after one when I dressed and went down to meet her when she arrived."

"You never left the inn?"

Boris shifted in his chair. "I was there when she arrived."

"And then?"

Boris looked at his lawyer, who sighed. "The question seems a little prurient. What Mr. Henry did after the time that interests you should be of no interest to you."

"The night man at the Jamison Inn says you showed up there after two and got the key to Kittock's room. He thought you were Kittock."

The lawyer sat forward, but Boris seemed undisturbed by the remark. "Roger can tell you why. Letters were missing from the archives. Letters of Father Zahm's. Well, I found them in Kittock's room, as I had thought I would. After his death, I thought there was no point in telling Greg Walsh who had taken them."

"You found the letters there?" Roger asked.

"That's right."

"Clare Healy can corroborate this, I suppose."

"For God's sake, leave her out of this."

This little outburst of gallantry brought an approving nod from Boris's lawyer.

"Now, about the plastic bag full of Kittock's effects that we found in your briefcase."

"What did you do, put it there before you asked me to get my briefcase? You must have noticed it in the car."

Foster shook his head slightly. Accusing the police was seldom a good tactic. "Doubtless you have looked for fingerprints on that bag or other indications that my client had handled it."

Jimmy just smiled. The fact was that there were none of Boris Henry's fingerprints at all on the bag. That Paul Lohman's and Clare Healy's had been found was adequately explained.

"I gather you drew a blank," Foster said.

"It doesn't matter one way or the other."

"Doesn't it? Lieutenant, your case against my client is flimsy in the extreme. You know he was in the Morris Inn when the crime was committed."

"I know he was sitting dressed in the lobby several hours afterward."

"Hardly an indictable offense. In any case, he has explained his presence. As for the slain man's effects, anyone might have put them into the briefcase."

"Why?"

"Why indeed? It seems to me that you have your work cut out for you. I must ask that you release my client."

Jacuzzi, the prosecutor, did not agree. "Look, when he went to the Jamison Inn and gained admission to Kittock's room, he knew the man wouldn't be there. And at that hour of the night? Come on. I'm going to arraign him."

When he did, Foster tried manfully to suppress his feeling that his client had fallen afoul of an inept small-town constabulary. Nonetheless, Boris Henry was bound over for trial. Bail was refused.

That evening the Knight brothers sat in their apartment with Jimmy Stewart and Greg Walsh. Jimmy understandably had the air of a man who had brought an investigation to a successful close. He and Phil reviewed the events leading up to Kittock's death much as had been done earlier during the interrogation of Boris Henry downtown. In the meantime, there had been added to the case against him that the shirts in his room were folded and in plastic bags of the kind that had been used to kill Kittock. One such bag was found in the wastebasket; then again, Henry changed shirts several times during the day.

"I've never seen Jacuzzi more confident," Jimmy said.

The review might have continued, but the game Jimmy had come to watch with Phil began, so they gave the television set their undivided attention. Roger and Greg withdrew to the study.

"In any case, the missing Zahm letters were returned," Greg said.

"Do you think Kittock took them?"

Greg thought about it. "He had been reading them in the archives. I suppose he thought it a mere peccadillo to borrow them so he could continue reading them in his room."

"I wonder where the Zahm diary is," Roger murmured.

Greg seemed surprisingly indifferent to the question, and Roger asked him why.

"It would not have ended up in the archives, Roger. If Henry has his way, there will be a Zahm Center. Our holdings will be raided, and, of course, the diary would go there."

"But now?"

"The administration has expressed deep interest in the idea."

"I doubt that there will be a Zahm Center now. I think the archives will get the diary."

"It is perhaps a fanciful thought, Roger, but Boris Henry seems capable of faking the theft in order to heighten interest in the diary and indirectly the center. When it reappeared, it would seem the very Q.E.D. for founding the center."

Roger smiled. "As you say, fanciful."

"But not impossible."

"The realm of possible things is a very commodious one, Greg."

It was the crack of dawn when Roger woke Phil the following morning. His brother emerged from sleep with difficulty, and the ravages of the previous night were visible in his unfocused and bewildered expression.

"What is it, Roger?"

"I've had an idea."

Phil fell back onto his pillow and groaned.

"It may very well be a wild idea, but until that is shown, I know I cannot rid myself of it. It has kept me awake."

When Roger explained what had been keeping him awake, Phil again made an exasperated sound, but then he seemed to remember how fruitful Roger's wild ideas had often proved in the past. Even so, he had reservations. "I can't call him at this ungodly hour, Roger."

"You could leave a message if he doesn't answer."

Phil squinted at the digital clock beside his bed. Annoyance gave way to a small, not quite evil smile. "Hand me the phone."

10 SORIN'S IS THE MAIN DINING room in the Morris Inn, named in honor of the founder of Notre Dame. On its walls, murals depict different historical periods of the university. Its large windows look out on an expanse of lawn and beyond to one of the new residences built on the erstwhile back nine of the Burke golf course. Roger Knight's luncheon party was placed at a large round table situated in a corner on the window side of the restaurant. The passage of the Hunneker Professor of Catholic Studies through the room caused diners to pause in their eating, conversations to stop, and expressions to register surprise and then awe. Behind Roger trailed his guests.

At the table, Roger carefully squeezed himself into his chair, while David Nobile and his daughter Rebecca, Paul Lohman, and Clare Hearly arranged themselves before him. The stated occasion for the luncheon was the arrival via Federal Express of the rare Lope de Vega volume David Nobile had purchased with Clare's aid. When they got settled, the precious book was produced and passed reverently around the circle. Roger ordered wine for his guests and when it was poured proposed a toast, his own being offered in ice water. This was done with exclamations of congratulation to Nobile.

"Now, David," Roger said, "I know you want to tell us all about your new acquisition, but the mere fact of it will have to suffice for our celebration."

"I wish I could feel more in the mood," Paul Lohman said.

"Ah, poor Boris," Roger said.

"It is uncanny how things have accumulated against him."

"He has an excellent lawyer."

"Do you think he will be acquitted?" Clare asked eagerly.

"His lawyer has every confidence."

"That is mock bravado, I fear," said David Nobile.

"If he is innocent," Rebecca said, "the search will have to go on for the one who did it."

"Exactly," Roger said. "A detective's work is never done."

"Do you yourself think he will get off?" Paul Lohman asked.

"I suppose it is more a hope."

"But if he is guilty?" David Nobile seemed to have reminded himself that they were talking about the death of his brother-in-law.

Rebecca said to Roger, "I still can't believe that you're a private investigator."

"It does strain credulity."

Paul Lohman persisted. "But hope has to have a basis, Roger."

Roger arranged his napkin over the expanse of his stomach and looked around the table. "Very well, let us discuss the matter *ex professo* and then put it behind us in deference to our reason for being here. What has happened and what do we know?"

Roger's narrative gift enabled him to give a capsule version of events that covered the main points, which he enumerated.

"First, there is the arrival on campus of Xavier Kittock to do research on Father Zahm in the archives. This interest was prompted by what Boris Henry had told him was contained in Father Zahm's diary, the actual location of the legendary El Dorado. Kittock was already bitten by the gold bug, having invested in and gone on an unsuccessful expedition to locate sunken Spanish gold off the coast of South America. His work in the archives seems clearly to have been aimed at finding out if there might be a clue there to what Zahm had put in his diary."

"Xavier had only Boris's word for what was in the diary," Clare said.

"That was sufficient for him to act on. Why would he doubt his old roommate?"

"Even if he were spoofing, the diary would still be invaluable," Paul Lohman said.

"And you think that its value as a rare book rather than the revelation of the site of El Dorado explains its theft?"

"I know I wouldn't mind having it," David Nobile said.

"Daddy!"

"Oh, I know it falls outside my central interest."

"That isn't what I meant."

"Second," Roger continued, "Boris arrives on campus and expresses displeasure when he learns what Kittock has been up to. His first reaction is to get Kittock banned from the archives by making it look as if he were purloining Zahm's letters. To that end, he himself takes the letters and puts them in Kittock's room."

"That isn't how it was," Clare said. "We looked for the letters, but they weren't there."

Roger looked pensive. "And yet when Jimmy Stewart and my brother visited the room after Kittock's body was found, the letters were there."

"Then Eggs did take them?" Paul Lohman said.

"Or Boris left them there when he and Clare visited the room in the hours just after Kittock was murdered."

Everyone turned to Clare in surprise. "The police know all this," she said, unruffled. "But the letters were not in the room when we looked."

"Point taken," Roger said. "No doubt it is the time before the murder that really matters."

"And the police found that Boris had been up and dressed until two o'clock." Clare's voice was heavy with sadness as she said this.

"Waiting for you to arrive from Chicago?"

Clare nodded.

"You phoned to tell him you were on your way?"

"Yes."

"What time was that, Clare?" Paul Lohman asked.

"I can't say exactly."

"No need to rely on memory," Roger said. "Your phone service keeps very accurate records."

"I suppose they do. In any case, it was some hours before I met Boris in the lobby of the Morris Inn, and that was two o'-clock."

"I'm told that the record includes both time and the place whence the call was made." Roger smiled around the table.

"What an odd world we live in. There is a surfeit of pointless information and a dearth of knowledge. Now, for our celebration. You placed the call from Chicago, Clare?"

"As you say, it must be recorded."

It was some fifteen minutes later that Clare excused herself. From his vantage point, Roger could see that Jimmy and Phil were waiting for her when she emerged from the restaurant. They said something to her, and she turned to go away, but Jimmy's hand closed on her arm. Then they went out of sight.

Later, Clare's absence was noted.

"I thought she was coming back," Rebecca said.

"The poor woman," Paul Lohman said. "You can't imagine how all this has affected her."

"I think I can," Roger said. "I think I can."

11 THE RECORDS OF THE CALLS MADE from Clare Healy's cell phone revealed that she had made the call to the Morris Inn from South Bend rather than from Chicago. Her plane from Kansas City had arrived at Midway at 8:00 P.M. Far more interesting was the call she had made to the Jamison Inn at 11:02 of the fateful night, a call to Xavier Kittock, also placed from South Bend.

"A rendezvous must have been arranged. Kittock arrived. He took a seat on a bench while he waited, and then his assailant crept up behind him and brought the plastic bag over his head."

"Clare?"

"Previously unidentified fingerprints on the bag turn out to be hers."

"But why on earth would she kill Eggs Kittock?"

"Because he had Father Zahm's diary."

"But the diary was found in Clare's suitcase."

"I used the past tense," Roger said. "It was to retrieve the diary and silence her ally that she killed Kittock."

"Her ally?"

"She made a number of calls to Kittock from Kansas City

"Forgive me, Roger, but if I never hear the name Zahm again it will be too soon."

"You're certainly right to think that several have taken his name in vain."

"Where did he stand on football?"

"Philip, what an interesting question. I'll look into it."

Marjorie Waters refused to believe that a woman could have the strength to kill a man that way.

Jim Casper disagreed. "Listen, I have known women—"

"I am not interested in the women you have known."

"Neither am I. Not anymore."

"Besides, interest is a two-way street."

"You want to give me driving lessons?"

Bernice exchanged a look with Ricardo, an old married couple watching the antics of the young.

"It's getting late," Bernice said.

"You're right," Jim Casper said. "I have to work tomorrow."

"And I have to work on my novel."

That brought Marjorie to her feet. For a moment she seemed to notice the difference in physical attractiveness between Jim and Ricardo, but then, as if accepting her fate, she put her arm through Jim's. They headed for the door.

"I don't know what he sees in her," Ricardo said when their guests were gone.

"Or vice versa."

A week later, Roger was in the archives with Greg Walsh examining the diary of Father Zahm.

"So the archives gets it after all," Roger said.

"Until and unless the university decides to go ahead with the Zahm Center."

"Perhaps the expense is in your favor."

Greg frowned. "Father Carmody thinks he has already secured a major donor. David Nobile!"

"Perhaps Mrs. Nobile will veto it."

"Who could persuade her to do that?"

Roger smiled. He had had a talk with Rebecca after class.

"I like him," she had said, meaning Greg Walsh.

"It would break his heart if the Zahm holdings, particularly the diary, were removed from the archives."

"My mother was livid when she heard how much Daddy spent for that Lope de Vega volume."

"The Zahm Center would involve a good deal more money."

"Well, I don't think they will get it from my father."

"What a relief that would be to Greg Walsh."

Roger could not believe that he was dishonoring the memory of Father Zahm in this matter. Would the great scholar and writer wish to be commemorated on the campus he had left so ignominiously after his term as provincial? Perhaps not. It was more difficult to imagine the priest liking the solution of the murder of Xavier Kittock. The fact that Foster was now exploring the possibility of a plea of temporary insanity for his client suggested that the lawyer knew what the outcome of a trial would be. It was an odd notion that a declaration of mental illness could make the freedom it secured desirable, but Roger's fundamental misgiving stemmed from the book in which Zahm had written movingly of the great women who had stood behind the great men of history. Of course, he must have guessed that a negative influence could be equally effective. Roger tried to develop this thought for Phil.

"They should never have released that maintenance man, Esperanza."

Father Carmody approved of such loyalty on Boris Henry's part. It seemed worthy of a Notre Dame man, however misplaced in this instance.

"It is the oldest rule in the world," he murmured. *"Cherchez la femme."*

"Why, you old chauvinist," Rebecca cried.

"My dear, you yourself have proved the point."

In a car parked overlooking the St. Joseph River, Larry Douglas sat with his arm around Kimberley's yielding shoulders, softly reciting the final stanza of "Dover Beach." "Ah, love, let us be true to one another . . ."

When he was finished, Kimberley lifted her face for his kiss.

"I told Feeney I'm coming back to work in the morgue."

"I thought you were just an intern."

"With a raise. I have to save money for medical school."

"Medical school."

"He'll groom me as his successor. He intends to oppose Jankowski in the primary."

"But that would take years."

"What's the alternative?"

He tightened his grip on her shoulders. "What Matthew Arnold wrote."

"You'll have to be more explicit."

So he was, and she accepted. Thus was a potential pathologist lost to the St. Joseph County morgue.

before coming here. Doubtless the plan to steal the diary was formulated then."

Boris Henry refused to believe the charges against his long-time assistant, even though they had effected his own release from jail. The services of Foster were transferred to Clare's defense. His calm assurance to the press that the case against Clare was no more solid than the risible one that had been advanced against Boris Henry was unpersuasive.

"But will it be unpersuasive to a jury?" Roger said.

"What jury will believe that a woman could have performed such a deed?" Boris said with disgust. His presence in the Knight apartment was equivocal, since he clearly regarded himself to be in the enemy camp.

"You mean physically?"

"Of course."

Rebecca joined in. "Oh, it's possible. We tested it." She smiled at Josh Daley. "Josh sat on a bench, and I crept up behind him and had the bag over his head just like that."

"He would have overpowered you," Boris said emphatically.

"That's what Josh thought. When he started to turn blue I removed the bag."

"Bah!"

"Mr. Henry, I never believed you could have killed my uncle. Your old friend, your former roommate . . ."

"Of course I didn't kill Eggs. But neither did Clare."

"Then who did?"

"Forgive me, Roger, but if I never hear the name Zahm again it will be too soon."

"You're certainly right to think that several have taken his name in vain."

"Where did he stand on football?"

"Philip, what an interesting question. I'll look into it."